CASUALTIES OF LOVE

'*A matter of life and death . . .* ' the stranger in the silver BMW told Joanna as he rushed off after saving her from what might have been a major accident. So perhaps it wasn't altogether surprising to discover that he was Giles Beltane, surgeon at Trinity Hospital where Joanna was staff-nurse. What was surprising was the impact the handsome surgeon had on her emotions . . .

CASUALTIES
OF LOVE

BY
GRACE READ

MILLS & BOON LIMITED
15-16 BROOK'S MEWS
LONDON W1A 1DR

First published in Great Britain 1987
by Mills & Boon Limited

© Grace Read 1987

Australian copyright 1987
Philippine copyright 1987

ISBN 0 263 75744 7

Set in Monotype Times 11.3 on 11.4 pt.
03-0587-45993

Typeset in Great Britain by
Associated Publishing Services
Printed and bound in Great Britain by
William Collins

CHAPTER ONE

As she approached the unmanned level crossing Joanna's car seemed, oddly, to be losing speed. Putting her foot down harder on the accelerator had no effect—her yellow Fiesta came to an abrupt and alarming halt in the dead centre of the railway track.

Joanna's stomach flipped. Hardly the best place in the world for your engine to stall! She slipped the gear-lever back into neutral and turned the ignition. All that produced was an ineffective rasping whine. To add to her troubles, the driver of the silver BMW, which had been sitting on her tail all the way from the petrol station, started tooting his horn.

'And you can belt up!' she muttered to herself, catching sight in her mirror of the hooter-happy character urging her to move, 'I'm not sitting here for the fun of it, for Pete's sake!'

There had been only one pump working at the small service station she had called at about five minutes earlier. Pulling up behind her, the man had leaned against his car while she filled her tank, impatience stamped on every inch of his powerful frame. Watching her every movement, his critical gaze had been decidedly off-putting. She had feigned not to notice and refused to be rushed. Affluent he might be, if his impeccable appearance was anything to go by, but he could jolly well wait his turn like everyone else.

Now, of course, it was a different story. Joanna was as anxious to get going as he was. Desperately she tried the ignition again and again without success. To her horror, the amber signal light at the side of the track came suddenly to life, followed almost at once by the undulating wail of the warning siren. *There was a train due!* Panic gripped her as she saw herself a sitting target in the path of the oncoming monster. What on earth could she do?

With trembling, frantic fingers Joanna fumbled to release her seat-belt. Nothing for it but to try pushing, if there was time. If not, she would have to abandon the car and fly for safety.

A door slammed behind her and to her immense relief she saw the tetchy horn-blower striding to her assistance. With an imperious wave of his arm he motioned her to stay at the wheel while he applied his muscles to the problem.

The amber light changed to flashing red as the Fiesta began to inch slowly forward. It rolled to safety with barely seconds to spare before the automatic barriers fell and closed the line.

Her palms sweating, her heart thudding painfully, Joanna steered in towards the kerb, where the car came to rest. She leaned forward over the steering wheel and rested her head on her arms, letting out a long sigh of thankfulness. She had never been so scared in her life. Phew!

A light tap on the window brought her out of her daze, and she was reminded that thanks were due. With words of gratitude forming in her mind she hastened to wind down the window. Before she could say a word, however, her rescuer barked:

'Are you tired of life, or something?'

Searching her pale face, his deep-set grey-green eyes were accusing. Joanna managed a wan smile, pushed back the soft hair from her clammy forehead and, in a voice that hardly seemed like her own, returned:

'I—I was beginning to think that life was tired of me! Thanks very much for your help. I'm most awfully grateful.'

'Hmmm.' The man's dark brows furrowed and he continued to study her in a most disconcerting fashion. Even though he was glowering, Joanna could not help thinking what an attractive face he had; more lean and rugged than classically handsome, with a pleasantly-shaped mouth that looked as if it turned up at the corners more often than down. At that moment, though, its line was severe and his deep voice disapproving: 'If you're going to run a car you should keep it properly serviced.'

'But I do. It's never played me up before. I don't know what's wrong. I'm not out of petrol . . . I just filled up.'

'Yes, I know. I was there,' the man said with heavy irony. His frowning gaze switched to his own car now isolated on the far side of the track. 'You seem determined to hold me up one way or another.'

'For goodness' sake!' Joanna protested, wide-eyed, 'I wasn't even aware of your existence until you started honking at me.'

They were both silent for a moment, she chewing her thumb nail, wondering what to do next, and he standing drumming his fingers on the roof of her car, effectively blocking her doorway.

Presently she said, 'Well, if you'll excuse me, please, may I get out? I'll have to find a phone and get the AA.'

The man turned his attention back to her predicament and stroked his firm chin thoughtfully. 'Just an idea . . . were you low on gas before you took some in?'

'As a matter of fact, yes, I was. I only just about made it to the garage in time.'

He promptly took his stylish, grey-suited self to the front of the Fiesta, placed the heels of his hands on the bonnet and gave it two or three vigorous shakes. 'Try it now,' he called, 'and make sure you're in neutral.'

His authoritative manner suggested a driving instructor and a very dim pupil. Joanna checked to make absolutely sure. It would have been too humiliating had she not been. He'd obviously decided she was a dumb blonde anyway. She turned the ignition key and the engine purred sweetly to life. 'Oh, that's amazing!' she exclaimed, delighted. 'How did you do that?'

'I imagine you got an air lock after letting your tank run dry. A good shake can often work wonders.' He gave her a meaningful glance and added wryly, 'and there's someone else I should very much like to give the same treatment. But for you, young woman, I could be where I should be by this time, not cooling my heels here wasting precious minutes.'

Now that her troubles were over her composure had returned. She flashed him her most disarming smile. 'I really am sorry about that. I hope it isn't terribly important.'

'Maybe a little matter of life and death.' He sighed in an exaggerated fashion but didn't volunteer any further explanation.

Joanna looked at him curiously. He reminded her vaguely of someone, but she couldn't think who. She said: 'You don't mean that, I hope.'

'So do I.' In the distance the sound of the approaching train could be heard, and he went on, 'Have you got your wits back well enough to drive?'

'Yes, I'm fine.'

'Off you go then, or you'll be holding me up yet again.'

'Perish the thought!' Joanna returned with an impish grin. 'Anyway, thanks again.' She went on her way hoping that the life-and-death remark was his idea of a joke. Anyway, she couldn't have held him up for more than ten minutes, could she? He'd probably said that just to heap coals of fire.

There was not far now to go before she reached the Nurses' Home. Still feeling a little wobbly after her close shave she drove with more than her usual care. Even before this hang-up she had been feeling somewhat below par. It was always unsettling meeting up with her volatile, extended family—the more so when saying goodbye to her mother who was off on her travels again. This time it was to Europe; a concert tour with the Orpheus Light Opera Company.

Joanna knew she should be used to it after all these years. Her growing-up had been peppered with comings and goings, and their relationship was a fragile but precious affair. Helen was not made for motherhood, although she had produced two daughters by different husbands and loved them both. Thank goodness for Aunt Beth who could be relied upon to look after the family home while everyone was away. That at least added some sort of stability to their otherwise chaotic life-style.

The silver BMW overtook her at speed and her knight errant gave her a casual toot in passing. Raising a smile, Joanna plucked a cheeky kiss from her lips and tossed it to him. How about that guy! Poised, self-assured, she'd like to bet nothing ever really shook his foundations.

Where was he bound for? she wondered. An important business meeting? A bit late for that, on a Saturday. A dinner date perhaps? Whoever and whatever he was he had certainly saved her skin— —might even have averted a major accident.

He had long since vanished from view before she came within sight of the complex of buildings which made up Trinity Hospital. The original solid structure was built of grey limestone blocks in the best Victorian tradition. It had since been extended to cope with the needs of a growing population and was now a medical centre of some repute in the Thames Valley area.

Joanna regarded it with affection as she passed by on her way to the Nurses' Home. Staffing on Paget Ward she had been really happy during the past six months. Sister Judd was a good manager, even if some of her ideas were outdated compared with St Martin's, the London hospital where Joanna had trained.

Life at Trinity was altogether more free and easy

than at St Martin's with its hidebound traditions from the year dot. True, it had been an excellent training and she had enjoyed being there, most of the time. Had it not been for her affair with Shaun Cassidy, one of the SHOs, she might even have stayed on in London.

She had made a complete ass of herself over that charmer, not wanting to believe that he hadn't a serious thought in his head. Maybe he had meant it when he'd said he loved her, but that didn't keep him faithful, which was no recipe for a secure and happy future. After she qualified Joanna finally did the sensible thing and put distance between them.

Love, she decided, was a dicey business. You were either on cloud nine or wallowing in misery. Thank goodness she was over Shaun now; she enjoyed being at Trinity and she was quite content just to pursue her career for the time being.

Turning down a wide tree-lined side road, Joanna made for the purpose-built Nurses' Home and parked her car behind it. Then, lugging her large zip-up travel bag from the back seat, she hauled it up to her room on the first floor.

It smelled rather stuffy after being shut up for a fortnight. Opening wide the casement window, she gazed out at the leafy gardens of the big houses opposite. Although nine o'clock, it was still not yet dark and the soft air was full of the sweet scents of late May. After the teeming life of the City it was pleasant to come back to this tranquil part of England with its attractive riverside towns and villages.

Music from a transistor drifted in from the open

window of the adjoining room. Pleased to find her neighbour at home, Joanna went next door, knocked and poked her head in. 'Hi, Gail!' she said brightly.

Clad in a pink towelling bathrobe, her friend sat blow-drying her long brown hair in front of the dressing-table mirror. 'Jo!' she exclaimed with a welcoming smile, 'am I glad to see you! I've had no one to moan to while you've been away. Want a coffee?'

'Okay. You finish your hair . . . I'll make it.' Joanna set about filling the electric kettle which lived on top of Gail's mini-fridge. She spooned coffee into mugs and made the drinks while they chatted non-stop. 'What do you have to moan about?' Joanna wanted to know.

'Oh, the usual. Shortage of staff and no shortage of patients. So how was your sister's wedding?'

'Great! Rachel looked terrific. All the cast of her musical were there and quite a few big names from the theatre. It was a whirlwind affair—she'd only known him a couple of months. I hope it lasts. Marriage in that world isn't exactly rock-solid, is it?'

Gail wrinkled her nose and sat herself cross-legged on a bean-bag cushion, her mug cupped between her hands. 'All those beautiful people, I suppose. Too much temptation. Have your folks left now, then?'

'No, early tomorrow. Beth will run them to the airport to link up with the rest of the company. It's a good thing they've got a tour manager to tie up the ends. They're completely scats, my mother and Malcolm. They'd forget their heads if it weren' for Aunt Beth.' Joanna sighed. 'Brussels, Hamburg, Budapest, Florence . . . sounds dreamy, doesn't it? Don't know why I missed out on the artistic talent.'

'Why . . . was your father a musician?'

'Yes, he plays a number of instruments; clarinet mostly. I see him occasionally, when he comes over here, but he spends most of his time in America these days. Goodness knows how they pupped me. All I ever wanted to be was a nurse. They think that's cute but kind of odd,' she smiled.

'Well, where would the talented be without the likes of us?' Gail said. 'At least no one could call you scatty. You're one of the most together people I know.'

Joanna made a wry face. 'Question of having to be when you've only got yourself to depend on. I'm a bundle of insecurities really. And I know one guy who wouldn't agree with you.' She went on to describe her encounter at the level crossing. 'There's a lot to be said for a good pair of biceps when you're in a tight spot.'

'There's a lot to be said for a good pair of biceps, period!' cracked Gail. 'Was he young, old, or indifferent?'

'Mmmm . . . ' Joanna pondered, 'in his thirties, I should say. Quite high-powered by the look of him. Used to issuing orders and having people jump to it. You know, the dominant male type. Anyway,' she added, 'what's been going on here? Anything interesting?'

'A few comings and goings. You knew about Prof James and his MI, didn't you?'

The grey-haired, urbane Professor James Beltane

had been Consultant Surgeon at Trinity for many years. 'Oh yes,' Joanna said, 'that happened before I went on holiday. How is he?'

'Made a good recovery. He's gone away to convalesce now. Don't suppose we'll see him back for some time, though—if ever. Still, we're chuffed with his stand-in.'

'Who's that?'

'His son, Giles. Looks like a younger edition of the old man, actually. Very personable, loads of machismo.'

Joanna snapped her fingers. 'That's who he reminded me of . . . '

'Who are you talking about?' asked Gail.

'The guy who pushed my car off the line. He was the dead spit of Prof James. He said he was on a life-or-death mission. I thought he was pulling my leg at the time, but I suppose he *could* have been on his way here to an emergency.'

'Well, you'll soon find out, won't you? You're bound to see plenty of Beltane Mark Two on Paget.'

'Ye-es,' Joanna said, thoughtfully. Then she giggled. 'I blew him a kiss when he overtook me.'

'That'll teach you! So what else did you get up to while you were away?'

'Oh, not a great deal. Went to a couple of parties with Adrian—he's Malcolm's son by his first wife—no relation to me really, but we treat each other like brother and sister. Then I bought some clothes, and saw some of my old mates from St Martin's and got all the latest scandal. You remember that SHO I almost got engaged to?' Gail nodded, and Joanna went on, looking pensive, 'well, he's not there now, either. I'm glad I woke up to him when I did.'

Memory conjured up the curly-haired, lovable Irishman with the roving eye. She had been so naïve. It had taken her some time to realise that Shaun had no intention of committing himself to any one girl in the foreseeable future. A stable, loving relationship was the last thing on his mind.

'Talking of changes,' Gail said, 'we've got a new gasman. He's not bad. And the bush telegraph's beginning to work quite well.'

'Oh, don't tell me you've fallen!' returned Joanna in mock despair. 'With the divorce rate being one in three and all that?'

'Simmer down . . . I'm not hearing wedding bells,' Gail chuckled. 'He just improves the scenery and adds a bit of spice to the daily grind. He's a cheeky devil, in a dry sort of way.'

'Sounds ominous to me.' Joanna finished her drink, stretched luxuriously and ran her fingers through her cloud of blonde hair. 'Well, this needs washing, and I promised to ring home to let them know I've arrived, so I'll love and leave you. What time are you on tomorrow?'

'Early.'

'Oh! I don't start till lunchtime.'

'There's a cocktail party in the doctors' mess tomorrow night,' Gail remembered. 'Coming?'

'What's that in aid of?'

'The Cas men in A & E got their heads together and decided they ought to get better acquainted with the rest of us. They are kind of insular, and I suppose it does help to oil the wheels, knowing who you're dealing with.'

'Mmmm . . . yes,' Joanna agreed. 'Depends how busy we are. If I'm not too shattered I'll come.'

Going along to the pay-phone in the corridor, she dialled her home number. It was her mother, Helen, who answered. They had the usual affectionate light-hearted exchange that marked these occasions, with deeper feelings being left unsaid. Words were inadequate to convey what Joanna really felt. It was almost as though their roles were reversed and her lovable, irrepressible mother was the child.

'Don't forget to send me postcards from wherever,' Joanna said in parting. 'Hope it's a good tour. My love to Malcolm. Take care of each other. 'Bye.'

With a resigned sigh she replaced the receiver and went back to her room to unpack and pick up the threads of her own life. Malcolm was her mother's third husband, whose own son Adrian was also making his mark in the theatre. Despite the fact that they all made a great fuss of Joanna on the few occasions when they met, she never felt as though she belonged. And seeing them and leaving them again only served to remind her of that fact.

The following afternoon Joanna reported for duty on Paget Ward. Clad in her pale blue uniform dress, navy belt around her slender waist, blue-bordered cap perched on her glossy hair, she presented a picture of glowing vitality.

Sister Judd greeted her staff nurse warmly. 'Hallo,

my dear. You look blooming. Did you have a
good holiday?'

'Yes, great, thank you, Sister. How's everything
with you?'

'Not too bad. Although I could have done with
four pairs of hands this morning.' Normally quite
serene, the older woman sounded a little ruffled.
'You can see we've no empty beds.' She nodded
her iron-grey head in the direction of the long,
busy ward.

An orderly was clearing away the last of the
lunch dishes, the nursing staff were scurrying
around getting routine jobs done and patients back
to bed before Sunday afternoon visiting. Sunday
was usually the intake day for waiting list admissions.

'There was a pile-up on the motorway last night,'
the Sister went on. 'We took three of the casualties
and we've had to put off three of the people who
were down for tomorrow's list. I hate having to do
that. It's so unsettling for them when they've made
arrangements and probably got themselves all
psyched up for the big moment. But there you are,
it couldn't be helped.' She gave a resigned shrug.

They had been joined by the rest of the afternoon shift. Leafing through the Kardex, Sister
Judd briefed them on the present state of the
patients, most of whom were new since Joanna
was last on duty.

'All last night's admissions are in High Dependency,' the Sister continued. 'Mrs Wells, fractured
ribs and left pneumothorax . . . she's comfortable
at the moment. Mrs Thomas, facial lacerations and
mild concussion . . . we're to keep an eye on her

for a couple of days. And young Lucy Rhodes . . . splenectomy and multiple abrasions . . . she's still rather poorly. The doctors will be up some time today to see them, I expect.' She glanced at Joanna. 'You knew about Professor Beltane, didn't you?'

'Yes. Tough luck that, wasn't it?'

'It was indeed . . . not had a day's illness all the time I've known him. Still, it seems to have been a fairly mild attack. If he behaves sensibly he should be all right, but you know doctors; not the best of patients, are they?' She handed the ward keys to Joanna. 'Well, I'll be away to my lunch now. There's the drugs still to do. Let young Carol assist with that, she needs the practice. And keep an eye on Lucy. Her next lot of blood is due about two. You'll have to send for some more.' With that she picked up her belongings and departed.

The nurses scattered to their appointed tasks and Joanna went in search of Carol, a second-year student, an urchin-faced girl with big brown eyes and a straight-fringed bob. She found her in the sluice putting a used bedpan into the macerator.

'Carol, would you like to come and do the drugs with me? Sister said you wanted the practice.'

'Oh, yes please, Jo.' The student nodded eagerly. 'I'll just wash my hands. Be with you in a jiff.'

The routine round gave Joanna the chance to familiarise herself with the patients as she made herself known to them and checked their medication sheets with the junior.

As one might have expected on Sister Judd's ward, everything was as it should be; except that Joanna was not too happy about the girl with the splenectomy. Having completed the drugs round and locked the trolley away, she left Carol to wash up the medicine measures while she went back to check on the patient.

The girl lay with her eyes closed, frowning as though in pain. There was a nasogastric tube taped to one side of her cheek and a blood transfusion dripping steadily into a vein in her forearm.

Joanna smoothed back a strand of damp brown hair from the pale face, and the twenty-year-old lifted heavy eyelids and managed a feeble smile.

'How's it going, Lucy?' Joanna asked gently, her fingers on the girl's rapid pulse. 'Are you in pain?'

'Not especially . . . I just feel . . . anyhow. I'm hot and my mouth tastes awful. Couldn't I have a drink?'

'Well, not yet, I'm afraid. We don't want you to be sick. I'll get you a mouthwash, and we'll give you a nice cool sponge down. That'll make you more comfortable.'

She went away to fetch a washing trolley and some clean linen, and collected Eunice—a good-natured SEN—to help her with the bed-bath. They worked well together, being gentle with the girl's sore spots and making sure that her dressing was intact, remaking the bed with fresh smooth sheets.

'There, that looks better,' Joanna smiled, plumping up a final pillow.

'Thanks,' Lucy said. 'I'll be glad to get rid of all these tubes.'

'You will soon,' Eunice encouraged, swishing back the screening curtains.

Having checked that the drip was still running properly, Joanna sent her helper to the Blood Bank for the further supply of cross-matched blood that would soon be needed.

She had cleared away the washing trolley and was back in the office and about to read up some case notes when the doctors arrived. The surgical registrar, Peter Green, was accompanied by his houseman, Steve Marks, both in their white coats. The third member of the party, in a smart fawn sports jacket and well-fitting brown cords, gave Joanna something of a jolt, although she was not entirely surprised to see him, in view of her talk with Gail the previous night.

Rising to greet them she stole a wary glance in the surgeon's direction and gave a half-smile. His dark brows lifted in surprise.

'Good afternoon, Jo,' Peter breezed. 'Sister not about?'

'No, she's at lunch. Can I help you?'

'Yes. Oh, I suppose you won't have met Mr Beltane yet,' Peter said, remembering she'd been away. 'This is Nurse Leigh, sir.'

'Well, well!' Giles Beltane murmured with mild amusement. 'The blue-eyed traffic stopper.'

'Sorry?' Peter looked slightly puzzled.

Joanna felt herself blushing as she explained: 'Actually we did meet, unofficially, yesterday. He gave me a hand when my car faded out on me.'

'Hmmm . . . yes . . . well, cars and women rarely understand each other, I find.' Giles Beltane paused for a moment and his dark-fringee lively eyes, meeting hers, gleamed wickedly. 'Well . . . shall we get on, then? You're probably aware that I prefer not to waste time.'

The other two doctors exchanged grins while

Joanna looked uncertainly from one to the other. 'Do you want to do a round?' she queried. It was, after all, Sunday afternoon with visitors due at any moment.

'No, no!' Beltane returned with an exaggerated show of patience. 'Just last night's RTAs, Nurse. Any problems?'

'No, I don't think so, although Lucy Rhodes' temperature is still up,' Joanna told him. 'We've just tried cooling her off with some tepid sponging.'

Light-footed, she led the way to the bedside. It was best to forget their earlier encounter, she decided. This newcomer might have a poor opinion of women drivers, but at least she should have no trouble proving herself an efficient nurse.

On the face of it that should have presented no difficulty since she loved her job and knew she was good at it. The problem was that during the course of his visit whenever his questing eyes met hers, she found herself as nervous as a first-year student. Which hardly fitted the calm, capable staff nurse image she intended to convey.

CHAPTER TWO

JOANNA was very glad that they had managed to see to Lucy before the doctors arrived. Although still woebegone, she at least looked a little better for having had her bed freshly made, her nightdress changed and her hair combed.

Giles Beltane greeted his patient in a friendly manner. 'Hallo, Miss Rhodes . . . and how are you feeling?'

She attempted a feeble smile. 'Rather bruised and battered, Doctor.'

'I'm not surprised, my dear. You've had a rough ride.' He laid his fingers on her pulse, then glanced across at Joanna. 'Have you checked the wound?'

The resonance of his deep voice and the magnetism in his dark-lashed eyes had an odd effect upon her equilibrium, but she replied in a confident voice, 'Yes, it's draining well. Would you like to see it?'

He nodded. 'Please.'

She drew her side of the screening curtains while Steve, the houseman, on the far side of the bed dealt with his.

Folding back the bed covers, Joanna raised Lucy's nightdress to expose the long subcostal incision. It was in good shape with no seepage into the dressing around the drain.

'That's fine,' Giles agreed. 'May I just listen to your tummy?' Clipping his stethoscope into hi ears he checked for signs of the returning bowel sounds. 'Good!' he remarked cheerfully, folding the instrument and putting it back into the pocket of his sports jacket. 'That seems to be in order. In a few days the soreness will go and you'll be feeling much better.'

Joanna rearranged the bedclothes and smiled at her patient.

Lucy looked at the doctors and began, a little self-consciously, 'Thank you . . . for looking after me. Sorry . . . I kept you all up half the night.'

The surgeon patted her hand. 'Just you concentrate on getting better, and that will make it all worthwhile. We can probably dispense with your nasogastric tube in the morning,' he added with a quiet smile, 'then you'll be able to start drinking.'

'How will it affect me, not having a spleen?' she wanted to know.

'Hardly at all. Your lymphatic system will take over the job it did.'

'Then, why do we have a spleen in the first place?'

A dimple flickered in Giles's lean cheek. 'Ah! Well, the human body can be amazingly adaptable when the need arises.'

He reached for her clipboard, flipped through the charts and conferred with the registrar. 'Let's see . . . she's on Ampicillin, and Pethidine for pain relief, and her haemoglobin's up to twelve now . . . ' Switching his attention to the blood transfusion stand, he eyed the emptying pack. 'You won't allow this to run out, will you?' he said, turning his gaze on Joanna.

'No, I've sent for some more. It'll be here soon.'

'Good. We mustn't risk any more air locks, must we?'

Joanna concentrated on tidying back the bed curtains without comment. She supposed he was entitled to his little dig, in the circumstances.

The doctors moved on to check that the other two previous night's casualties were progressing satisfactorily and then gathered in the office for a private discussion.

'Nice girl, Lucy Rhodes,' Peter said. 'She's a bright kid. Sad about the boy-friend.'

'Why? What happened to him?' Joanna asked.

'He was driving the car they were in. He died.'

Her eyes rounded with compassion. 'Oh dear! I didn't know that. I haven't had time yet to catch up on all the details.'

Appending a few notes to the case files Giles Beltane observed shortly, 'Lethal weapons, motor cars.'

A disturbing thought nagged at Joanna. If she hadn't delayed him, might he have been able to save the boy? That was something she certainly wouldn't want on her conscience.

Sister Judd returned from lunch just then and joined in the dialogue. Eunice also came back with the fresh supply of cross-matched blood and Joanna excused herself and went off to change the pack.

'Here we are, Lucy,' she said, 'just what the doctor ordered.'

It was fairly obvious that the girl, although putting on a brave public face, had been shedding a few tears since they left her. And not without good cause, Joanna now realised. She busied herself clamping off the tube above the drip chamber replacing the old pack with the new and taking time to readjust the flow. She stayed watching the drip for a moment, not wanting to intrude but feeling moved to sympathise.

'Lucy,' she began gently, 'I've only just heard the bad news, about your boy-friend. I'm terribly sorry.'

The girl's lips trembled. 'Th-they said it was for the best . . . b-but, oh! it's so *unfair,*' she choked.

'Yes, I know . . . it must be awful for you.' Joanna paused, a lump in her own throat. 'How did it happen?'

'Oh, s-some speed merchant overtook us,' Lucy quavered, her lips trembling. 'He crashed head-on into another car . . . we ploughed into that lot . . . Tony was trapped b-behind the wheel.'

Now that she had begun she seemed glad to talk, and Joanna listened, murmuring the occasional word of sympathy. Bottled up grief, she knew, could only make matters worse. Far better to let it out if other people would allow you. She learned that the boy had been a medical student, which somehow seemed to make it all the more poignant. Every white coat was probably a reminder of a promising future cut short.

Visitors had started to trickle in and a middle-aged woman headed in their direction, carrying a bunch of pink roses.

'Oh, here's my mother,' Lucy murmured, sniffing back her tears and blowing her nose. 'Don't want her to see me upset . . .'

Joanna turned to greet the parent. 'Hallo, Mrs Rhodes,' she said, 'the doctors have just been to see Lucy. They're quite pleased with her progress.'

'Yes, I just had a word with them,' the woman answered, her expression anxious all the same. She bent to kiss her daughter. 'How are you, love?'

Lucy had put on her brave face again. 'Not too bad, Mum. Mmmm . . . lovely roses!'

'Yes, gorgeous, aren't they?' Joanna enthused. 'I'll find a vase and put them in water for you.' She smiled and left the two of them together.

The stems of the blooms were very thorny. Handling them was not without its hazards, as Joanna found when she stripped off some of the leaves to make arranging easier, and pricked her fingers in the process. After taking back the flowers to the ward she returned to the office before going for her tea break.

By this time the doctors had gone and Sister Judd sat at her desk sorting through some paperwork.

'Ah, Joanna,' she said, rooting in her greying hair with the end of her pen, 'there's a first-year straight out of introductory block starting tomorrow morning. Now, I'm on days off, so you will make sure she gets looked after, won't you?'

'Yes, of course, Sister.'

'Good. I know I can rely on you. It's important to make these learners welcome and show them the proper way to go about things. We shouldn't expect them to muddle through without back-up.' Sister Judd regarded the future standards of the nursing profession as her personal responsibility.

Joanna smiled to herself, but nodded. 'One's first ward can be a pretty scary experience. Don' worry, we'll look after her.' She inspected an esp cially sore place on her index finger, and then sucked it.

'What have you done to that?' Sister Judd asked.

'Oh, nothing much. I just pricked it on one of Lucy's roses. There were some wicked thorns on the stems. Well, I'll go for my tea now, shall I?'

'Yes, righty-ho, dear. The others have gone.'

At the counter of the Friends' Coffee Shop, Joanna was joined by the houseman who had been on the ward earlier. They collected their drinks and sat at a table together.

'Good to see you back, Jo. We missed you,' Steve told her. 'Paget isn't the same without your cheerful face.'

'Pull the other one!' She peeled the wrapping off her Kit-Kat, broke it into fingers and offered him one.

'It's true!' he said, between bites. 'Not that there's been much to be cheerful about lately. Past two before I got to bed this morning . . . I've been wandering around like a zombie all day. And there's GB still galvanised for action—it's positively sickening, after last night's mayhem.'

Joanna stirred her coffee thoughtfully. 'That multiple RTA, you mean?'

'Mmmm . . . A & E was snowed under. Two people went to Neuro and three to Orthopods, besides those on your ward.'

'That girl's boy-friend . . . what exactly happened to him?'

'Massive internal injuries. He was DOA. Nothing much anyone could have done anyway . . . not even wonder-boy Giles.'

'Oh, I see.' In spite of feeling sad for Lucy, a

feeling of relief surged through Joanna. If the man had been dead on arrival then it had nothing to do with the surgeon being delayed for a few minutes. 'How are you getting on with Beltane?' she asked. 'Find him okay?'

'Yes, fine. Really on the ball. Doesn't treat the rest of us like morons, either.'

'Neither should he, if he wants co-operation. I can't stand doctors with exalted opinions of themselves.'

Steve looked at her askance and grinned. 'That sounds shirty, coming from the good-natured Jo. I thought I sensed an atmosphere between the two of you on the ward.'

'Oh, you're imagining things,' she said. 'I just thought he was a bit pleased with himself.'

He chuckled. 'Whatever he is, no one else seems to mind. He's got all the theatre staff pandering to his every whim. Mind you, he's not a ladies' man, so take warning. If you boob, feminine wiles will get you nowhere.' He helped himself to her last chocolate finger. 'You didn't want this, did you?'

'All the same if I did. And I don't play the helpless female, as you well know,' she returned with a grin.

'Just a friendly word, doll. I wouldn't like you to get your little heart broken. He does seem to have some kind of fascination for the fair sex. You coming to the A & E party tonight?'

Joanna pursed her lips noncommitally. 'Gail did mention that, but I'll see how I feel by the end of the day.'

'Oh, come on, force yourself. We ought to encourage initiative. We should all mix more.'

'I thought you were supposed to be flaked out?'

'We—ell, nothing like a bit of riotous living for putting the zizz back into you.'

'Okay, you've talked me into it,' she smiled. 'I could do with some cheerful company after thinking about Lucy's problems.'

With Sister Judd and the rest of the early shift going off at four-thirty, that left just three nurses and an auxiliary to cope with the busy evening routine. Joanna put on a plastic apron and got down to the necessary dressings and other skilled procedures, while Eunice and Carol dispensed the drugs and the auxiliary took round the supper trays.

When suppers were cleared away everyone lent a hand with getting patients back to bed and making them comfortable for the night. Then, amid frequent interruptions from the ever-busy telephone, Joanna set about writing her handover report.

At nine o'clock the night staff duly arrived in the shape of Staff Nurse Delphine Dupont and a third-year student. Both looked daisy-fresh in contrast to the day nurses at the end of their labours. Having deposited their belongings in the staff room they joined Joanna in the office to hear about the state of the ward. Then the third-year ambled off to see about the late-night milky drinks while the two senior nurses had a few last words.

'You'll find two more packs of Lucy's blood in the fridge,' Joanna said, passing over the ward keys. 'That should see you through all right, and with no empty beds it should be a bit more peaceful than it was last night.'

Delphine, a vivacious, dark-eyed French girl, spread her hands and shrugged in Gallic fashion. 'I 'ope so!' she said in her fractured English. 'Like Paris in ze rush hour it was 'ere. Mad! All ze patients waking up and wanting things. *C'est la vie*, huh?' she sighed.

'Stopped you from dropping off, anyway,' Joanna laughed. 'Well, I'm away. I promised Steve to show up at the A & E drinks do tonight.'

'Oh, give 'im my love. 'E was a good boy last night . . . ' Delphine's eyes sparkled suddenly, 'and what about our Mr Giles, huh? 'E is the dog's whiskers!'

'You mean "the cat's whiskers", you chump. But I shouldn't go overboard for him. Apparently women don't figure where he's concerned.'

'Ah! Maybe 'e don't like to mix business and pleasure, but . . . ' Delphine wagged a knowing finger, ' 'e is a red-blooded man, no?'

'Yes, he's that all right,' Joanna grinned. ' 'Bye, now. See you in the morning.'

Drawing her blue-lined navy cloak about her shoulders she set off back for the Nurses' Home, and her thoughts returned briefly to that other red-blooded doctor, Shaun Cassidy, who had played havoc with her affections. Thrown into contact, often in quite intimate situations, it had been all too easy for the persuasive Irishman to sweep an impressionable young nurse off her feet. Thank goodness she was not likely to make that mistake again. And if Giles Beltane was the kind who preferred to keep things on a professional basis, then that was fine by her.

Joanna made time for a shower to freshen herself up before dressing for the evening. She decided on wearing her silky black trousers and teamed it with a scarlet camisole top. Then she combed her gleaming fair hair back at the sides and caught it up behind with a thin black ribbon. After adding eye-shadow, blusher, some lip gloss and a pair of pearl stud ear-rings, she checked her overall image in the mirror and began to feel in real party mood.

The doctors' mess was attached to the Residency at the rear of the hospital. By taking a short cut through the car-park it was barely five minutes' walk from the Nurses' Home. Slipping into her matching black silk jacket, Joanna stepped out blithely in the soft night air towards the lighted building.

Pushing through the swing-doors of the mess she paused to seek out familiar faces in the crowded room. Loud pop music, voices and laughter vied with each other and a general air of mateyness abounded.

A jovial dark-bearded character came towards her. 'Hi!' he breezed, 'you look a bit lost. I'm sure I've seen you around . . .   Alex Hill, I'm one of the casualty officers.'

Joanna smiled and said, 'Hallo, Alex. I'm Joanna Leigh—I'm from Paget Ward.'

'Ah! That explains it. You're one of the reasons for all this socialising. So that we can get to know some of the ward staff better. Do you know anyone in A & E?'

'No, not really. A few by sight, although I've probably spoken to some of you on the phone.'

'Right. Let's find you a drink and get better

acquainted.' He took her elbow and led her in the direction of the bar which was being manned by two of the hosts. 'John, meet Joanna,' Alex said. 'She's from Paget Ward. John is our senior charge nurse,' he went on to explain, 'without whom we should all be up the creek without a paddle.'

The charge nurse beamed at her through gold-rimmed spectacles. 'Believe that and you'll believe anything, Joanna. Anyway, glad you could come. Champagne cocktail?' He filled a glass with sparkling wine, added a dash of brandy and passed it over. 'That's the prescription for tonight. We're all letting our hair down.'

Leaning against the bar and nibbling at peanuts, the casualty officer studied her with interest as she sipped her drink. 'Are you a product of Trinity?'

'No, I've been here about six months now. I trained at St Martin's.'

'Oh, you're one of *that* mob. Not a bad scene, but not a patch on the GCH, of course.'

'I suppose that's where you were?' she smiled.

John nodded. 'A buddy of mine went to Martin's as an SHO. You might have come across him . . . know Shaun Cassidy?'

Joanna nearly choked on her drink. He patted her on the back and grinned. 'Does that answer my question?'

'Yes,' she said wryly, on recovering. 'I knew Shaun.'

'He was a bit of a Romeo at GCH. Still sowing his wild oats, was he?'

This was all she needed . . . the ghost of Shaun to pop up just when she thought he was well and truly buried. 'I did hear he'd moved on from there now,' she said.

The charge nurse brought an end to the subject by enquiring about the previous night's casualties. 'Three of them went to your ward, didn't they? How's that lass with the ruptured spleen?'

'Lucy Rhodes . . . she's okay. Shattered about losing her guy, though.'

'That's the trouble with Casualty work,' Alex put in, 'half the time you never hear what becomes of the people you scrape off the deck. Still, neither do you have time to bleed for them, so I suppose it's as broad as it's long.'

They continued to talk shop until Alex's attention was claimed elsewhere and Steve came to seek Joanna.

'I'd almost given you up,' he said. 'Come and dance.'

Finding a space they began to swing to the compulsive rhythm of the disco music.

'By the way, Delphine sent you her love,' Joanna remembered. 'She said you were "good" last night, whatever that may mean,' she added impishly.

He raised an eyebrow. 'She did, did she? It might be worth my while to pop back there later then.'

'I thought you were supposed to be tired out after last night's work load?'

'Not too tired to miss an opportunity when it arises.'

'Men! All tarred with the same brush, aren't you?' she said in mock despair.

'Do I detect a note of cynicism?'

She wrinkled her nose at him. 'Let's say I couldn't have survived in this jungle without waking up to a few of the facts of life.'

'It's the old Adam in us, sweetheart,' Steve sighed. 'Can't fight nature, can you?'

'So what happened to willpower?'

'Will Power? Who's he? Never heard of the guy.'

Joanna giggled. 'All right, funny man. Go and chance your luck with Delphine and I'll find someone more sensible to talk to.'

They finished their dance and Steve said: 'Actually I am on call, Jo, so I'd better look in on the wards in case there's anything needed. Be back later . . . so long.'

Joanna saw Gail with some of the people from Theatre. She went over to join them and was welcomed into the lighthearted group. With them was the new anaesthetist, Dorian Hardy, a man in his early thirties with a prematurely receding hairline. His rather mournful face had a kind of whimsical humour about it.

'And what is your claim to fame, Joanna?' he enquired with casual interest.

'Oh, I haven't one. I just keep a low profile and try to stay out of trouble,' she returned flippantly.

'My sentiments exactly.' He paused, his eyes sliding over her neat figure in its black and red outfit and the soft fair hair contrasting with her darker curling lashes. 'You don't look much like a shrinking violet if I may say so.' Looking past her, he went on, 'And here's someone else who scarcely fits that description. Evening, Giles.'

Everyone turned to greet the surgeon who approached them. Joanna herself had been well aware of the moment Giles Beltane had entered the room. He was too powerful a figure to go unnoticed. She had glimpsed him to-ing and fro-ing and making himself generally agreeable. All the same, she felt a queer sensation in the pit of her stomach when he actually came over to speak to them.

Greetings were exchanged and, after a few preliminaries, Joanna suddenly found herself the focus of his attention. His lively eyes sought hers. 'So you've been on holiday, have you? Where did you go?'

'Oh, just home this time,' she replied. 'We had a wedding in the family.'

'And where is home?' he prompted.

'Chelsea.' Under his steady scrutiny her pulse began to quicken. She launched into further explanation purely to relieve her tension. 'We had the reception on a boat on the Thames. It was really terrific.'

'Oh, that must be the in thing these days,' put in Tasmin, the Theatre Sister. 'Wasn't there a singer who recently got married and had her nuptials afloat? Rachel Gibson?'

'Yes . . . Rachel's my sister,' Joanna admitted with a slight smile. 'It was a very show-bizzy affair.' Dropping her gaze, she briefly inspected the sore place on her finger before sucking it.

'You and your sister aren't much alike then?' Giles queried.

'Well, she's my half-sister really. But no, I'm the cuckoo in the nest. All my family are in the entertainment world except me.'

It seemed somehow to have turned into a conversation between the two of them, as though the others were merely interested bystanders in an intensely personal situation. She studied her finger again. 'What's the matter with that?' he asked.

'I pricked it on a rose thorn this afternoon.'

'Let me see.' He reached for her hand and examined it closely. The unexpected action both disturbed and embarrassed her. 'There's still something in there,' he went on, stretching the skin around a black speck in the pad of her forefinger. 'Anyone got a needle?'

Tasmin laughed. 'Not on me. It's not the kind of thing you bring to cocktail parties.'

Joanna tried to pull her hand away. 'It's nothing. I'll have a go at it when I get home.'

'Let's do it now. Come on over to A & E.'

She raised her eyes to heaven, 'No . . . for goodness' sake! There's no need to make such a fuss over a little thing like that.'

'Little things can cause big problems. Move!' Giles turned her by the shoulders in the direction of the doors and marched her out. A ripple of laughter followed them.

'That was an unnecessary show of force, wasn't it?' she protested. 'You made me feel a complete idiot.'

'You *were* a complete idiot. You should have come quietly and no one would have batted an eyelid.' He held her hand in a firm grasp, pulling her towards the lighted hospital buildings. 'I assume you have had an anti-tetanus injection?'

'Yes,' she snapped. 'And I object to being ordered about.'

'Dear me! A rebel spirit. That should make life interesting.'

She could think of no crushing rejoinder. Doubt-

less she would in half-an-hour's time, which would
be a fat lot of use since she intended to get this
over as quickly as possible. 'You can let go my
hand,' she said with dignity. 'I'm not thinking of
making a bolt for it.'

'Sensible girl!' Giles drawled, but he didn't release
her until they had pushed through the swing-doors
into Casualty.

At this hour of the night the department was
quiet with just a couple of people in the waiting
area and no one on the reception desk. On hearing
their footsteps in the corridor, a nurse poked her
head out of the treatment room.

'Hallo, Mr Beltane,' she said, surprised. 'Can I
help you?'

He gave her a disarming smile. 'No, thank you,
Nurse. We can manage. Just going to get a splinter
out of a finger.'

She smiled curiously from one to the other
before going back to her work.

Giles ushered Joanna into another cubicle and
nodded to a chair. 'Sit down.'

With a resigned sigh she sat, while he took a
hypodermic needle pack from a trolley and stripped
off the wrapping. Then, holding her injured finger
firmly between his own he probed deeply at the
black speck until he brought it out. 'There you
are, there's the culprit.' He showed it to her before
dabbing the place with antiseptic. 'Now, suppose
you stop gritting your teeth and say thank you.

'Thank you,' she returned, primly, and got up
to leave.

He restrained a wry smile. 'If I remember rightly,

you threw me a kiss the last time I performed a service for you.'

'That was before I knew who you were.'

'And if you'd known who I was, would that have made a difference?'

'Probably not,' she said pertly. 'It was just a reflex action, anyway.'

'I see . . . and there was I thinking you were truly grateful!' He paused, picked up both her hands and inspected them. 'Why do you bite your nails? Does the work worry you?'

She might have known he'd notice that! Pulling them away, she plunged them into her jacket pockets. 'No, it doesn't. And I don't . . . not all the time. Only when I've got . . . things on my mind.'

Joanna had no wish to prolong this tête-à-tête. She resented his self-assurance and paternalistic attitude. It had been an enjoyable evening until his intervention. Now she felt thoroughly uncomfortable and out of sorts. 'Shall we go?' she said.

'Okay . . . I'll take you back to the party.'

She was certainly not going back there at *his* say-so. Glancing pointedly at her watch she said, 'There's not much point. They'll probably be packing up soon. I'm calling it a day . . . I'm on an early tomorrow.'

'As you like.'

They walked away from the quiet confines of the department. The sky was a high, black star-studded vault as they stepped out into the soft night air. A soothing breeze cooled Joanna's pink cheeks but had no effect at all on the upheaval inside her. But it was a relief to be free of the claustrophobic atmosphere in the treatment room. The intimacy of the situation had made her ill at ease.

She turned in the direction of the car-park. Her high heels tapping along the tarmac sounded extraordinarily loud. Giles strolled nonchalantly alongside her, within touching distance, but with his hands thrust into his trouser pockets.

'You came in your own car, did you?' he asked.

'No, I walked. I live at the Nurses' Home.'

'Oh, then I suppose I'd better come along with you.'

'Really, there's no need. It isn't far,' Joanna protested.

'And how do you think *I* should feel if you met with some dreadful disaster after we parted?'

She fought back a giggle, her sense of the ridiculous returning. 'Relieved, probably, to have me out of your hair. That's if it bothered you at all,' she quipped.

'Hmmm.' He flashed her an appraising sideways glance. 'I'm not given to cheering the demise of even my worst enemies, let alone tiresome little nurses.' They walked in silence for a few moments before he went on, 'Do you like living in the Nurses' Home?'

'It's not bad . . . it's convenient, for the time being.' Now that their clash of wills had subsided and he seemed to be agreeable, she saw no point in not reciprocating. 'In London,' she expanded, 'I used to share a flat with friends, which was nicer.' She paused to look up at the powerful figure of the man beside her, his angled features softened by the darkness. 'Where were you before you came here?'

'In the Middle East for a time.'

'Was it your father's illness that brought you back?'

'No, I was already back. I was due to join him here in any case, which was rather convenient. I must say, after the carnage of the Lebanon it makes one appreciate this green and pleasant land.'

'I'm sure . . . and there are some gorgeous spots along the river, aren't there? The water fascinates me—maybe because I'm an Aquarian,' she added, joking.

He laughed. 'Don't tell me you go along with all that rubbish?'

'Oh, I always read my horoscope,' she returned flippantly. 'If it's good it sets me up for the day. If it's bad, then I don't believe it.'

'And that's feminine logic, is it?' They were by now back at the entrance to the Nurses' Home. 'Well, I do hope your stars have good news for you in the morning, for everyone's sake. Goodnight, Joanna.' With a condescending grin, he turned to go back the way they had come.

For a moment her eyes lingered on his broad shoulders and the sensual grace of his long legs as he strode away. Then she ran up to her room thinking disparaging thoughts about supercilious surgeons.

It was very clear, though, what Steve had meant about Giles Beltane's appeal to women. There was an undeniable something about him. Dominant characters could be fascinating. More so if they combined toughness with that touch of gentleness he had shown towards Lucy. It was the small considerations that made inroads into one's defences. And if he'd been working in the Lebanon that also showed concern for the helpless population of a strife-torn country.

Well, forewarned was forearmed. He posed no threat to Joanna. Her heart was not up for grabs by James Bond types who threw their weight about, but there was no reason why they shouldn't have a satisfactory working relationship.

All was quiet as she walked along the lighted corridor where vague cooking smells still lingered in the air. She let herself into her room, discarded her finery and washed off her make-up. After searching out a clean uniform ready for the morning, she was about to go to bed when there was a tap on her door.

Gail looked in. 'Oh, you're back, are you?' she said, her brown eyes curious. 'We couldn't imagine what on earth Giles was doing with you.'

'Nothing to make the headlines, I can assure you. He just dug out my thorn and I decided it was too late to go back to the party.'

Gail made a comic face. 'Anti-climax, eh? Well, there you go. Great party, though, wasn't it? What did you think of Dorian?'

'Mmmm . . . he seems okay.'

'That's a bit lukewarm.'

Joanna smiled. 'You know me . . . extremely cautious since my last experience with a medic. But don't let me put you off.' She patted a yawn. 'Look, I must go to bed or I'll need a kick start in the morning.'

'Well, I did have something else to tell you. But it can wait. 'Bye.'

After setting her alarm for seven Joanna tumbled into bed for what remained of the night. For a while she lay wakeful, her brain busy with the events of the day, especially the latter part. Peculiar how that man seemed to have dominated her affairs ever since her return to the hospital.

In fact until tonight, when the subject had cropped up at the party, even family matters had faded into the background. Rachel's wedding, and her mother and Malcolm setting off on their tour; normally her head would have been full of it. She always felt nostalgic after seeing them all. This time, however, there had been too much else to think about.

Tomorrow, with Sister Judd being off duty, another busy day lay ahead of her. She supposed Giles Beltane might look in after his outpatient clinic, to sort out who could be discharged, to free a few beds. In a way she was rather looking forward to it.

Demanding though he was, and irritatingly self-confident, Joanna felt she had survived their encounters today reasonably well. But he obviously was used to having his own way. It might be good for him, meeting someone who was not prepared to humour him. With a smile on her lips, she fell asleep.

CHAPTER THREE

BEING in charge of the ward for the next couple of days left Joanna little time for thinking about much else but the work.

The new first-year student, Sally Armstrong, had arrived and needed to be looked after. Joanna could well remember what it was like to be a new girl on your first ward. The moment of panic, not knowing what would be expected of you and wondering if you would measure up.

'Hallo, Sally,' she said, greeting the nervous eighteen-year-old with a friendly smile. 'You'll be working with Beryl today. If there's anything you don't understand, don't be afraid to ask.'

Beryl Baines was a level-headed third-year student shortly to take her Final, and Joanna went on to detail the work. 'Will you make a start on Lucy? Her Ryle's tube is to come out this morning and she can sit out while her bed's made. You can tell Sally all about her while you're getting the things together, can't you?'

'Yes, okay, Jo. Come on, Sally, we'll need plastic aprons. I'll show you where everything's kept.' Explaining as she went, Beryl took her protégée off towards the equipment room.

Satisfied that the newcomer was in safe hands, Joanna got down to her paperwork. She filled in diet sheets, made out the drugs requisition, attached Path Lab reports to case notes and checked that specimens for analysis were ready for collection.

It was an averagely busy morning. The nurses went about their routine tasks of bathings, pressure care and bedmaking, dressings. The Path Lab ladies arrived with their trolley to take required blood samples. The physiotherapist came to give deep-breathing exercises to chesty patients. Porters delivered post and ferried patients to and from X-Ray. The ward-maid dispensed mid-morning drinks and helped patients find their money for the man delivering newspapers.

Lunches were being served before the doctors put in an appearance. With no medical school attached to Trinity Hospital, ward rounds were not the high-powered affairs they had been in Joanna's student days. At St Martin's the consultant and his team had been accompanied by a posse of medical students.

Today there was only the surgical registrar, Peter Green, accompanied by Steve. Joanna was relieved, in a way, that Giles Beltane was not with them. She was glad of a breather before having to encounter him again after last night's little rumpus.

'Hallo! You do choose your moments,' she said.

'What? Oh, lunchtime, is it? Sorry about that,' grinned Peter. 'The vasectomy clinic was popular this morning.'

The round was a leisurely business with the registrar apologising to patients for interrupting their meal. It ended with the usual discourse in the office over cups of tea.

Making notes on three of the case files, Peter laid them to one side. 'These patients can go as soon as they can make arrangements. That wil free the beds for the people we had to put off at the weekend. Giles's secretary will be getting in touch with them.' He stirred his drink and paused to take a mouthful before going on:

'There's a Mr George Montagu downstairs who Giles wants admitted. Abdo pains for investigation. They're keeping him in the day ward until you've got a bed ready.'

'Will GB be up later then?' Joanna queried.

'I shouldn't think so. He had to shoot off . . . a lecture to the School of Nursing, he said.'

'There'll be a few more moonstruck dollybirds about after that,' remarked Steve.

Joanna laughed. 'What makes you think we're all so vulnerable to a few muscles with a macho image?'

'Well, aren't you?' he returned audaciously.

'The scales dropped from my eyes many moons ago,' she told him. 'Well, you guys, if that's all I can do for you, can I get on?'

Peter levered himself out of his chair. 'Okay . . . let them know about that bed for Mr Montagu.'

Steve slid off his perch on a corner of the desk, gave her a broad wink and departed with the registrar.

With the arrival of the second shift, the early nurses went to lunch. Joanna got held up by a telephone enquiry. Then she was waylaid by the clinical tutor who wanted to arrange a ward teaching session for her pupil nurses.

In the canteen Gail was already halfway through her meal by the time Joanna arrived. She collected a quiche and salad and went over to join her friend. 'What was it you were going to tell me last night?' she asked, squeezing mayonnaise on to her salad. 'Anything important?'

Gail said, 'How would you fancy sharing a furnished house with me?'

Joanna's eyes widened. 'Why . . . have you heard of something?'

'Yes, it's near Pangbourne—belongs to a married cousin of mine.' Gail paused to finish the last mouthful of her egg on toast. 'Her husband is being transferred to Holland soon, on business. They'd rather let it to me at a lower rent than risk not being able to get strangers out when they want it back.'

'Oh, that sounds terrific!' enthused Joanna.

'Yes, and it's quite convenient. Only a couple of stations down the line . . . about twenty minutes by road.'

'Great! When is it going to be available?'

'Well, I'm not quite sure yet, but I promised to go over at the weekend and talk about it. When are you free?'

'Sunday afternoon?' Joanna giggled at a random thought and Gail wanted to know what was funny.

'I just remembered something that happened when GB walked me home last night. I said something about reading my horoscope, and he took the mickey. I only said it in fun, but I did read my stars in someone's paper this morning and it said a *change of scene is indicated.*'

Gail grinned. 'He certainly wasn't having any argument from you last night, was he? Nobody, but nobody says no to our Giles.'

Joanna frowned. 'Bet there were a few snid

remarks when he hauled me off like that.'

'No, as a matter of fact, that's where you're wrong. Dorian told us Giles is quite paranoid about infection hazards. It appears his wife died of septicaemia after tearing her leg on some barbed wire.'

Joanna was surprised and shocked. 'Oh dear! That's sad,' she murmured, turning it over in her mind. 'When did this happen?'

'About a couple of years back. Dorian and he were together at the Radcliffe at the time.'

'I wonder if that's what made him take off to the Middle East . . . to forget,' Joanna said thoughtfully. Perhaps last night he wasn't just being officious after all. He'd been taking precautions following bitter personal experience.

Gail glanced at her watch. 'Well, time I was back. I'll ring my cousin Pam and say we'll be over on Sunday, then, eh?'

'Yes, fine.' Joanna stayed to finish her coffee before going back to her work, half thrilled about the prospect of living out, half preoccupied with what she had heard about Giles. You never knew, she reflected, what made people the way they were.

The rest of the day flew by. The three patients for discharge were collected by their relatives. She sent them off with Outpatient appointment cards and wished them well, and felt inordinately gratified when seventy-year-old Mr Smith—who'd had a successful prostatectomy—insisted on kissing her goodbye.

When the spare beds had been disinfected and made up fresh, she phoned through to A & E to say that it was now convenient to send up the Mr

Montagu who was waiting in their day ward.

'Hallo, Joanna!' said a voice she now recognised as John, the senior charge nurse. 'Didn't see the going of you last night. Did you enjoy our party?'

'Yes, I did, John. It was really great. And it's nice to know who I'm talking to at last,' she said with a smile in her voice.

'I second that. We're thinking of making it a regular thing.'

They had just concluded their business when a policeman appeared in the entrance to the office and tapped on the glass. He enquired after Lucy, wanting to know if she was up to being interviewed about the accident.

'I don't want to worry her before she's ready, only it's as well to get a few facts straight while they're fresh in the mind, so to speak.'

'Oh! I see. Just a moment . . . I'll go and check,' Joanna said.

He seemed a pleasant enough man and she thought it might be best to get it over with, since it had to be done. Lucy, beginning to feel better, raised no objection and Joanna returned to the policeman to give him permission.

'Go easy on her, won't you? She's been through a bad time, what with her guy being killed . . . '

He nodded. 'Yes, Nurse, I know. I'll be the soul of discretion, I promise you.'

Showing him to the bedside, she gave him a chair, looked at her watch and decided to keep an eye on his length of stay. Ten minutes later, glancing in their direction, she was glad to see them getting on quite well. He had put his note-book away and was just sitting chatting to the girl in a kindly fashion. He rose to go and waved Joanna a cheery goodbye on his way out.

She went along to see how Lucy had coped. 'Everything all right? He seemed a decent sort of chap, didn't he? I hope it didn't make you feel bad, going over it all again.'

'A bit,' Lucy said, 'but he was really nice, and I'd do anything to get that road-hog convicted.' Her bottom lip began to quiver and she caught it between her teeth.

Joanna straightened a pillow which was slipping. 'Well, you've done your bit now,' she comforted, 'so try not to think about it.'

'I can't help it. The rotten part is, it was my fault we were on that road at all. Friends of mine had invited us to a party. Tony never liked them very much. He only agreed to go to please me . . .'

'Oh, Lucy, you mustn't think like that!' Joanna returned. 'There are times in everybody's life when they could say if I hadn't done this, that wouldn't have happened. It was just the luck of the draw . . . no fault of yours.'

'Yes, I suppose so,' Lucy sighed. She caught Joanna's hand. 'Thanks for being so nice to me . . . I do appreciate it. I always feel better after talking to you.'

Joanna grinned. 'I wish they'd all say that! Anyway, it's easy to be nice to the nice ones.'

'Why, do you get many of the other kind?'

'A few. But when people are ill they often behave out of character, so we don't take it personally.' She took a sniff at a vase of freesias on Lucy's locker. 'Mmmm . . . aren't these gorgeous? Well,

I'm off now. See you tomorrow. Be good.'

It was by now four-thirty and after handing over the ward keys to the second shift staff nurse, Joanna went off duty with the rest of the early shift. In the corridor she fell into step beside Sally, the new student. 'Well, how did it go today?' she asked.

'Oh, smashing. I thought I'd be general dogsbody, just doing bedpans and making beds, but I did quite a lot of things, and some of the patients were really sweet to me.'

Beryl exchanged smiles with Joanna and said, 'You got let down lightly today. The great awakening cometh!'

'We all have to do our share of the dogsbodying,' Joanna added. 'Join the club.'

Outside it was a mild, early June afternoon with sunlight warming the grey-stone hospital buildings. Approaching the rose-brick addition of the School of Nursing lecture hall, she found herself thinking of Giles and his lecture. A number of student nurses were drifting from the building with their notebooks. Judging by their cheerful demeanour, they had clearly not been bored.

Some lectures Joanna had attended, given by learned professors, had been positively yawn-making. GB, she felt, was hardly likely to be in that category. For a start his voice was rich and compelling, and he was certainly articulate; no waffling. Coupled with which he was good to look at. The problem might be if susceptible young nurses focused on the man rather than his message. Steve might well have a point there.

She said hallo to a couple of girls who had

worked on Paget Ward and then hurried on to the Nurses' Home, not wanting to risk bumping into Giles should he still be around.

She found herself thinking of the tragedy in his life, and then of the tragedy in Lucy's life. Joanna had finished with Shaun because there was no security in a future with him. But even if you had security it could be finished off by one stroke of bad luck. Perhaps one should live for today and let tomorrow take care of itself. That's what her mother did . . . but she was only happy in fits and starts. There had been great traumas when the split came with her husbands. Joanna came to the conclusion that love was a veritable minefield and certainly no guarantee of roses all the way.

Gail had made it back before her and had already changed into jeans and a sweat shirt. She made coffee and sat and gossiped while Joanna discarded her own uniform and put on a pink cotton jumpsuit.

'I've phoned my cousin,' Gail said, 'and it's okay for Sunday . . . I said about five, because she has to go out in the evening.'

'Fine. It'll be terrific, having a whole house to spread ourselves in, and to have our friends back whenever we like. Well, what shall we do tonight, Gail?'

'Oh, nothing energetic. My feet have had it today.'

So they decided on going out for a take-away and coming back for a lazy evening watching television.

Joanna made the acquaintance of Mr Montagu the

following day. He had been operated on overnight for a twisted gut. Delphine reported that he had been returned to the ward at four a.m. and was still sleeping off the effects of his Omnopon.

' 'E is very shocked,' she said, 'and dehydrated, and pyrexial. They did an anastomosis. We will have trouble wiz him!' she forecast darkly. ' 'E don't seem good.'

When Joanna did her round Mr Montagu, a hollow-eyed man with flushed, sunken cheeks, was awake and complaining bitterly. 'You, *Nurse!* How long do I have to put up with this bloody pain before you do something about it?' he whined. 'I want a drink . . . why can't I have a drink? And take some of these blasted bedclothes off me! It's like an oven in 'ere!'

'Yes, all right Mr Montagu,' Joanna said, soothingly. 'I'll be giving you an injection in just a minute, and we'll give you a wash and sit you up a bit. That will make you feel more comfortable.'

'I'm not sitting up for you or anyone else . . . I feel too bad. You go and get that injection or I'll report you to the matron . . . get a move on.'

Joanna could see that they were indeed going to have trouble with this one. But she felt pity for him—the man was very ill. There had been signs of peritonitis.

His wife arrived during the morning and sat with him and listened to his complaints until he fell asleep. Then she apologised tearfully for his behaviour. 'He does have a bit of a quick temper, and I know you do your best, but he's not himself at the moment.'

'Don't worry, Mrs Montagu,' Joanna said, 'we

do understand. Now, you haven't had a very happy night either, have you? Come and have a cup of tea before you go home.'

She put a comforting arm around the woman's shoulders and led her to a chair in the day room.

Later, Peter and Steve came to take stock of their patient and Peter pulled a dubious face as he studied the temperature chart.

'Was it Giles who operated?' Joanna asked.

'Yep. The loop was gangrenous. He's having all the antibiotic cover we can give him, but . . . ' and the registrar shrugged.

Joanna was pleased to see Sister Judd back the following day and to hand over responsibility to the older woman. The Sister had an air of authority to which even the most difficult of patients yielded. But as the week went by Mr Montagu slipped into delirium. He became comatose and finally died in the small hours of Friday.

One way and another it had been a difficult week. Joanna was not sorry to see the end of it. Mr Montagu had been one of their failures. His wife was left a pitiful and bewildered lady. It depressed them all, including the doctors.

Joanna knew that Giles had been in and out of the ward repeatedly but it so happened that she had never been around at the time. She could imagine that he, too, would be disappointed at his failure.

It was a welcome break when Sunday arrived and she and Gail set off to visit her cousin to arrange about renting the house.

They used Gail's car, since she knew the way. After leaving the town, a short journey through

country roads brought them to the attractive
Thames-side town of Pangbourne. Passing through
the central area with its fine old buildings and
foaming weir, Gail turned her Volkswagen in the
direction of a small housing development on the
outskirts.

'Here we are,' she said, pulling to a halt outside
a cottage-style villa in a quiet close.

It had a red-tiled roof, whitewashed walls and
diamond-paned leaded windows. It was called
Swallows and was one of eight similar houses with
open-plan front lawns.

'Nice!' said Joanna, releasing her seat-belt.

'Yes . . . they've only been married a couple
of years. This is their first home, which is why
they're anxious to have the right people in it.'

Gail pipped on her horn which brought her
cousin Pam to the door to greet them. 'Hi!' she
said, smiling from one to the other. 'Come on in.'

She led the way into a comfortable but modestly
furnished living-room, and they sat down to talk
over a cup of tea before she showed them around.

'Jim won't be back till late tonight,' Pam said,
'but we can fix things up between us now, if you
like. I'm leaving all the linen and enough crockery
for everyday use, but I'll pack away some of our
wedding presents and put them in the box room,
if you don't mind.'

'Oh yes, I'm sure that's best,' Joanna agreed.
'We shouldn't like to damage anything.'

She paused at the sound of a distant metallic
click, then jumped when a sleek dynamo of cream
fur shot past her across the room. It ran up the
curtains and sat peering down at them from its

perch on the pelmet, blue eyes blinking—a Cheshire cat without the grin.

Pam laughed. 'Oh, meet Willow. That's the one wedding present I can't put away. He goes with the house I'm afraid. He's no trouble . . . I'll leave a supply of food. You wouldn't mind looking after him?'

Both girls agreed that was fine by them and they'd enjoy having a pet around. That settled, Gail's cousin went on to show them the house.

The small kitchen had chartreuse mottled-tiled walls, formica-topped work surfaces and was fully equipped with aids to modern living. At the top of the stairs there were two fair-sized bedrooms, a box room and a bathroom in avocado green.

The couple expected to be leaving within a fortnight. 'When we come back we'd let you know beforehand so that you could look for something else,' Pam said.

'No problem,' Gail replied. 'If the worst came to the worst we could always move back into the Nurses' Home.'

Having agreed on the rent which the girls would pay monthly by banker's order, they were all very pleased with the arrangement. Pam waved them off from the front door after promising to let them know when they could move in.

It was that most fragrant time of the year between late spring and early summer. The hedge-rows were heavy with white blossom and lilac blended its heady perfume with the scent of the first roses.

'Oh, I'm so thrilled.' Joanna sighed with bliss. 'Let's go somewhere and celebrate.'

'Yes, why not? There's a smashing pub at Goring. We'll go there.'

Within five minutes she was parking the car in the gravelled courtyard at the back of an ancient hostelry. Down by the riverside gardens white-painted wrought-iron tables and chairs stood invitingly on the green lawns. Huge willows overhung the wide, peaceful stretch of water where ducks and coots were busy about their own affairs. On the far bank smart cabin cruisers sat at anchor in their private moorings at the bottom of gardens.

Treating themselves to a long, cool Pimm's, the girls carried their drinks to an outside table and sat and admired the view. In front of the low, picturesque inn the flagged terrace was bordered with multi-hued irises. To one side of the sweeping lawns a rustic arbour supported climbing roses. From the nearby weir came the sound of rushing water.

'Isn't this heavenly?' Joanna said.

'Yes, the only thing missing is a handsome hero to whisk us away and make mad, passionate love in his cabin cruiser,' Gail dramatised.

'Oh, that would spoil everything . . . the serpent popping up in Eden. Seriously though, I must admit I kind of envy your cousin her nice little love nest. I'm almost persuaded domesticity might not be bad if you found the right man.'

'Catch-22! Well, I'm a super optimist,' said Gail. 'You never know who's round the corner.'

At that moment things were fine as they were to Joanna. She liked her job, she had some good friends, and her bad patch over Shaun was a thing of the past.

The evening air was sweet with the scent of the roses. There was one variety with moon-yellow single flowers and bright orange stamens, and Joanna could not resist going over to smell them. The wickedly thorny stems reminded her of her encounter with Giles Beltane, and she was careful to avoid them.

'That one was called Mermaid,' she said, coming back to the table after reading the label. 'Gorgeous, isn't it?'

Gail was only half listening. Her attention was focused on the restaurant doorway from which two men in neat lounge suits had emerged. Deep in conversation they began ambling across the grass. 'If I'm not mistaken,' she said slowly, 'isn't that GB?'

'Where?' Joanna turned to look, and then she caught her breath. But it was not so much the sight of Giles Beltane which sent goose pimples over her scalp. It was his companion, the slightly shorter man with curly brown hair.

As if by telepathy both men glanced in their direction. Recognition was obviously mutual. They paused, exchanged a few words, then Giles and Shaun Cassidy began walking over to where the girls sat.

Joanna closed her eyes in dismay. 'Oh no! I don't believe it!' she muttered under her breath.

CHAPTER FOUR

GAIL took one look at Joanna's panic-stricken face and laughed. 'No need to look so petrified just because Giles decides to come over and say hallo.'

'It's not *him* I'm worried about,' Joanna returned, with a sinking feeling.

There was no time for explanation, because Shaun was advancing towards her, a broad grin on his Puckish face. 'Well, well!' he exclaimed. 'This is a turn up!' and he bent down and kissed her.

She hid her embarrassment behind astonishment. 'Shaun! Whatever brings you here?'

'I'm in general practice now, in this area. Mr Beltane tells me you're both at Trinity,' he went on including Gail in his smile.

Outwardly unperturbed, Joanna made the introductions and Gail made the appropriate noises. Apart from greeting both girls politely, Giles let his ebullient companion do most of the talking. But briefly meeting his candid gaze, Joanna sensed he felt her tension; it was almost as though they were telepathic.

Inwardly, she groaned. Of all the appalling luck! With the whole country to choose from Shaun *would* have to decide to settle here.

'Have you two known each other long?' she asked, making an effort to be bright and sociable.

'No, not long. We met at the local GP Committee,' Giles explained. 'I understand you knew Cassidy at St Martin's?'

'Yes, we were very good friends, weren't we Jo?' Shaun raised an eyebrow and studied her with critical amusement. 'You've been at it again, I see.'

Her mouth opened. 'At what?' she queried defensively, wondering what he was about to come out with.

'Smelling the flowers. There's pollen all over your nose.' He chuckled and brushed off the bright yellow dust with his forefinger. It was an intimate kind of gesture, and her cheeks flushed.

Shaun ruffled her hair playfully, said he was really pleased to see her again, and asked was this a favourite haunt of theirs?'

'No, not really,' Joanna said.

Gail explained: 'We're just celebrating the fact that we're going to rent a house not far from here.'

'Oh, that's great! I'll expect to be invited to the house-warming.'

Giles glanced pointedly at his watch. 'Dr Cassidy, I think we ought to cut this reunion short, if I'm to see your patient . . . '

'Yes, of course. Sorry Jo, must go. We'll catch up with each other later, hm? I'll be in touch now I know where to find you.'

After saying their goodbyes, the two doctors departed.

With a despairing sigh, Joanna ran her hands through her blonde locks. 'You know who that was, don't you?'

'Yes, it did get through to me,' returned Gail. 'He's the guy you broke up with. Seems rather nice, and he was genuinely pleased to see you. What went wrong?'

'Oh, just about everything. Yes, he *is* nice, and we had some great times, but he's a real woman-iser. I told him I wasn't sharing him with half the nursing staff. He said I was too possessive. I told him to push off . . . and he did.'

'You didn't think he'd take you at your word?'

'No. And my pride was hurt, I suppose,' Joanna admitted. 'It was the only thing to do though. What future is there with a man you can't trust, however much you like him? I came here to get away from him. And the last thing I want is to have my past raked up in medical circles here.'

'We-ell, if they met to see a patient, I can't see Giles getting side-tracked into gossiping about other people's love affairs. He's not that sort.'

'Mmmm, maybe you're right.' Joanna chewed her lip.

'Did it upset you, seeing him again?' Gail queried.

'Well, not really . . . apart from the shock. I'm not in love with him any more. I've got over that. At the time you don't think you ever will, but you do.' It had been a welcome surprise to find that there was no tug at her heartstrings, no desire to be in his arms again. Merely embarrass-ment. So that was one blessing; and whatever Shaun's faults she didn't really think he was the kind to kiss and tell.

In any case, their paths were hardly likely to cross unless he went out of his way to make them. And as Gail had reminded her, Giles Beltane was far too wrapped up in professional matters to concern himself over such trifles. She shrugged her shoulders. 'Oh well, water over the weir . . . I've grown a second skin since those days.'

The idyllic riverside scene had begun to pall. 'Let's go back,' she said. 'Perhaps we can get in a game of tennis, if we can find a court free.'

They finished their drinks and returned to the car. 'That wasn't a bad idea of his though,' Gail said, driving back to the Nurses' Home. 'About having a house-warming party when we move in, I mean.'

Joanna agreed. 'Any excuse for a party . . . and we don't have to invite him, do we?'

Feeling quite optimistic about the future, they changed into tennis gear and made for the courts behind the medical residency. The two hard courts were both in play, one occupied by a foursome and the other by Steve and Dorian playing a singles.

The girls sat down on a grassy bank outside the nets and waved to the men. 'Going to be long?' Gail called.

'No . . . we're only fooling around,' Dorian called back. 'Come and join us.'

None of them were top-flight players but they had a light-hearted, hilarious knock-up and afterwards went over to the mess for some refreshment. As always there was a constant flow of hospital staff drifting in and out. Usually voices had to be raised to compete with canned music, but on this summer evening for a change the hi-fi was silent.

An upright piano which had seen better days was serving as a receptacle for used glasses. Joanna put her own glass down, raised the lid over the keyboard and struck a few chords. 'Not a bad tone this, is it?'

'Are we in for a bit of culture, then?' Dorian quipped.

'Yes, come on, give us a tune,' Steve prompted, and he pulled out the stool for her.

'Oh! I haven't played for ages.' She sat down and experimented a bit to loosen up. Then her hands slipped into a remembered medley from the musical *Oliver*. Her half-sister had once starred in it and, helping her to rehearse, Joanna had become quite familiar with the score. A small crowd gathered around the piano. Someone removed the empty glasses and lifted the top. They began to sing along with the catchy tunes, clapping appreciatively and calling for more when she finished.

'Sorry, that's your lot,' Joanna laughed. 'That's all I can remember apart from Hymns Ancient and Modern.' She closed the lid. One thing her theatre family background had taught her was that it was better to leave people wanting more than to risk being a bore.

What she hadn't realised until she turned round was that Giles Beltane had come in and was amongst the listeners. Catching her eye, there was a humorous quirk to his lips, as though he saw her as a precocious youngster who'd been showing off. And she imagined she must look rather juvenile, still dressed in her short tennis skirt.

'Hey!' said Gail, 'you're a dark horse, Jo. I thought you said you'd missed out on the artistic talent?'

Joanna gave a self-conscious smile. 'Oh, let's face it, I'm only a hack.' She had never enjoyed being in the spotlight and didn't relish it now, especially with Giles Beltane watching her with that satirical smirk on his face.

She jumped up and looked around. 'I thought I had a drink somewhere?'

'I'll get you another,' said Dorian. 'Rum and Coke, was it?'

'Just Coke, please.'

The cluster of people who had been around the piano began to wander off and Gail and Steve followed Dorian to the bar. That left Joanna with Giles, and she could think of absolutely nothing to say. He had that effect upon her. She was very aware of his powerful physical attraction. It aroused earthy impulses in her which were rather disturbing.

He leaned against the piano, his manner still mildly amused. 'Quite a surprise packet, aren't you?' he murmured.

'Am I?' She met his studied gaze with an assumed indifference totally at odds with her wayward thoughts. 'Well, I suppose that figures, since you know nothing at all about me.'

'On the contrary, considering our brief acquaintance I know a great deal about you.'

He began to check facts off on his long fingers: 'Your family have a home in Chelsea. They're all in showbusiness except you. You have a half-sister . . . which means that either your mother or father has remarried. You trained at St Martin's where you met Cassidy. And like most women, you're a menace in a car . . . '

'I beg your pardon!' she interrupted indignantly. 'It's a proven fact that women drivers have a far better safety record than men.'

He chose to ignore that and carried on: 'Apparently you're addicted to smelling flowers. You're going to be sharing a house with Gail. And you're an Aquarian. How's that for starters? Shall I continue?'

'Okay, okay!' Joanna had to smile. 'All *that* proves is that you've got a computer-like memory.'

She was glad that the others coming back with the drinks called a halt to that particular line of chat and the conversation became general.

Referring to their meeting by the river that afternoon Gail asked why Dr Cassidy's patient couldn't have been seen at the hospital.

'Oh, she's a thyrotoxic young woman,' Giles explained. 'Apt to get agitated and easily upset. She'd been on antithyroid drugs, but she needed to be seen fairly urgently. I'm taking her in for a partial thyroidectomy.'

The doctors became engrossed in a discussion on symptoms and possible post-operative complications of exophthalmic goitre, and the nurses decided to leave them to it.

'That was quite a successful day, I'd say. Wouldn't you?' Gail remarked as they strolled back towards the Nurses' Home.

'What? Oh, you mean about the house. Yes, great!' That particular matter had slipped to the back of Joanna's mind, what with meeting Shaun, and then her absurd kind of exchange with Giles. He certainly did seem to have noted a good many facts about her. Not that there was any special significance in that. His professional training would have taught him to be observant and remember details. He could probably have given similar run-downs on all his colleagues.

As to that, there were a fair number of things she had learned about him in their short acquaintance. He'd worked at the Radcliffe with Dorian . . . he'd lost his wife in tragic circumstances . . . he'd practised in the Lebanon . . . he understood cars . . . he was short on patience . . . but not above putting himself out for people. And with his dedication to his career, he would likely go to the top like his father.

So she had best put clamps on that physical excitement he stirred in her. He might choose to indulge in the occasional bit of leg-pulling with her, but that didn't mean a thing. No point in letting herself get interested in the guy. She didn't want a repetition of the Shaun affair, did she?

Gail was rabbiting on about all the advantages of private living arrangements; getting right away from the hospital off duty; being able to have friends to stay and throwing the occasional party; being able to make decent meals instead of having take-aways or canteen food. 'I'll be able to watch my diet,' she said, smoothing the slight bulge above her waistline. 'Not that you've anything to worry about. You never seem to put on an ounce whatever you eat.'

In the corridor the communal telephone was ringing as the girls arrived on the first floor. Gail ran to pick it up, spoke for a moment and then held it out to Joanna: 'It's for you-hoo!'

'Hallo, Joanna?' said a male voice. 'Know who this is?'

Her eyes widened. 'Is that you, Dad?' she ventured.

'Got it in one. You're very elusive, my dear. This is the third time I've tried to get you today . . . '

Joanna was laughing with surprise and delight. She hadn't spoken to her father since he had rung St Martin's from Texas a year ago to congratulate her on qualifying. 'Where are you?'

'On your doorstep, honey. We're over here for a summer season . . . doing a number of one-night stands. It was Oxford last week, Reading this. Haven't much time to spare, but I'd love to see you. Could we meet for dinner tomorrow?'

'Oh yes, Dad. That would be terrific. It's been for ever, hasn't it?'

' 'Fraid so, Jo-jo. My fault, I know. How are you?'

'Fine . . . and you?'

'Bearing up. I reached the big five-O this year, you know. Phoned Chelsea and had a gas to Beth. Your mother's away . . . '

'Yes, she's on the Continent . . . back in three weeks I think. Will you still be here?'

'Mmmm . . . can't say. Well, about our meal . . . I'm staying at the Chiltern Hotel. Could you make it over here, say about seven tomorrow?'

'Great, I'll be there,' Joanna said eagerly.

'Okay, Jo-jo. All the gen when we meet. Must go now. 'Bye, honey.'

Joanna skipped away from the telephone to tell Gail her news. 'That was my father,' she said, her eyes sparkling.

Gail looked blank. 'What, phoning from the States?'

'No, he's here to work. I'm meeting him for dinner tomorrow.'

She could hardly sleep that night for excitement. She had kidded herself that she didn't care that he hardly ever contacted her, that he never remembered her birthday although she always remembered his. It gave her a warm glow to think he'd bothered to get in touch at last. And she hadn't been called Jo-jo for years. It stirred up distant memories of childhood, when love was a warm kiss goodnight and the house had been full of her parents' music. That was long before she had known about the other kinds of love which could separate families.

The Chiltern Hotel was a rather splendid old-world inn with a riverside setting. Floodlights concealed in willows and silver birches lit up its white stucco walls and blackened beams. It was a popular venue for conferences and business entertaining as well as being the haunt of the more prosperous inhabitants of the county.

Joanna parked her Fiesta in the paved courtyard among the Jaguars, Rovers and other prestige cars. She was wearing a slim-fitting silky dress in soft rose-pink. She had put up her hair for the occasion and her jewellery was a single rope of pearls. Quite a few heads turned when she walked into the cocktail lounge. She did not immediately recognise anyone, but in any case, it was only just seven o'clock.

It was six years since she had actually seen her father in the flesh, so he was bound to have changed a bit since then. But that craggy face and the bushy brown hair and eyebrows would be distinctive enough, despite the passage of time.

Feeling conspicuous, Joanna wandered through on to the paved terrace by the water where people sat at tables over cocktails. No familiar face there, either, although she caught the drawl of American voices from a group of trendily-dressed visitors.

Going back into the cocktail lounge, she sat down to wait on one of the yellow silk-brocade settees. And she waited, and she waited. It was seven forty-five before he came strolling into the lounge accompanied by a sophisticated young woman, long auburn hair floating about her shoulders.

He was much the same as she remembered, except that his hair was peppered with grey and his waistline a little thicker above the close-fitting trousers of his blue linen suit.

He glanced around the room. Joanna rose, half-hesitantly, then his lean cheeks creased into corrugated laughter-lines, and with arms outstretched, he loped across to greet her.

'Jo-jo! My! You're quite a woman now, aren't you?' he boomed, kissing her affectionately on the mouth. No apology for being late . . . and she could smell the whisky on his breath.

'Hallo, Dad,' she said, smiling, although her spirits fell somewhat to find they were not alone. 'I was beginning to think I'd come to the wrong place.'

'What? Oh, have you been here long? It was Kay held me up in the bathroom, wasn't it, sugar?'

The red-haired 'sugar', standing by with a

patiently-sweet smile on her carefully made-up face, said in a soft Southern accent, 'Aren't you going to introduce me, Eddie?'

He put an affectionate arm around both of them. 'Joanna, this is Kay, my beautiful wife of one month. Kay . . . meet my lovely daughter. I told you she was something else, didn't I? Imagine me having two such gorgeous dames in my life.'

The girls brushed cheeks and Kay drawled in a little-girl voice, 'I'm *so* glad to meet you. Eddie has told me such a lot about you . . . and I do so admire nurses.'

It took Joanna a moment to get her breath back. She swallowed and did a double take. 'Y-you're just married? Oh! Congratulations. Dad, why didn't you tell me?'

Her father winked. 'Thought I'd surprise you. Well now, I want you two girls to be great friends. When we get back to Texas and get our house straight, you must come and visit us. She'll go down a bomb back home, won't she, Kay? The little English rose, eh?'

The hovering waiter gave them the dinner menus and took their order for drinks.

It was far and away the worst evening that Joanna had ever spent. She forced herself to be gay and agreeable, but to find her father married to a girl who was young enough to be her sister was no joke. It was shattering.

She had been looking forward to a lovely evening, just the two of them, catching up on the important details of their lives, instead of which everything was superficial and meaningless. How could you talk about family things in the presence of a stranger? And her father seemed like a stranger too, as though there were no blood ties between them despite his show of affection.

It transpired that Kay was a singer with the band. At least that might ensure that this marriage would not suffer the strain of separation, like some of the others, Joanna mused. There had been a fair number of women in Ed Leigh's life since he had broken up with Joanna's mother. This girl did seem a warm person, anxious to please, and some girls did prefer older men. Perhaps this time it would last. But the gap must be . . . twenty-five years . . . ?

By ten o'clock Joanna had had enough. Her face ached with the effort of smiling and the conversation seemed to be flagging. She glanced at her watch. 'Well, time I was getting back, I'm afraid. But I'm so glad we were able to meet. It's been really lovely seeing you both.'

Oh! Must you go? All right, honey. Shall I call you a taxi?'

'No, I've got my car outside.'

They walked with her to the car-park and stood talking for a few more minutes.

'Why don't you get a job in the States?' Kay suggested, 'then we could see more of each other.'

'Yeah, good idea, Kay. Jo-jo, we're playing the Regency Centre on Wednesday night. Try and make it, eh? Bring a friend and come backstage to see us afterwards,' her father said. 'I'll leave a couple of tickets for you at the box office.'

Joanna said she didn't know whether she could manage it, but she'd try. They parted with kisses all round and extravagant expressions of affection.

Driving back to the Nurses' Home she had never felt more miserable. Her father was hopeless—lovable, but hopeless. He hadn't the faintest inkling of what 'till death us do part' meant. It was all instant satisfaction . . . no staying power. A bit like Shaun in a way. Oh, to hell with the whole business of sex and love. She was far better off staying single. As for going to his wretched concert, why bother? He never even thought about her from one year to another.

Swinging her Fiesta sharply into the car-park, she narrowly missed the silver BMW which screeched to a halt, swerving to avoid her.

She backed into a gap, got out, slammed her car door and locked it, too full of her own miseries to think about anything else.

The driver of the BMW had also got out. He strode over to where she was. 'I thought that was you!' Giles Beltane glared. 'Thank your lucky stars I've got good brakes. Women have a better safety record than men, she said! Well, that's a laugh.'

If he had been expecting the usual feisty comeback to that, he was due for a surprise. Joanna burst into tears.

CHAPTER FIVE

'OH, shut up!' Joanna gulped, the tears running down her cheeks, 'we missed, didn't we?'

'No thanks to you!' Giles's strong face was steely. 'You were driving like a maniac. And it's no use snivelling either—that cuts no ice with me.'

'Oh, get lost! I-I've had about all I can take tonight, without this . . . '

She made to rush past him, but he caught at her arm to prevent her. 'All right, all right. Calm down. What's wrong . . . quarrelled with your boyfriend?'

'No, I haven't,' she flared, struggling to get free, 'I've been having dinner with my father . . . '

'Oh! I *see*.'

'You don't. You don't see at all.' The tears came afresh. 'Let me go.'

'In this state? My dear girl, I'm not a sadist,' Giles said with resigned patience. 'Come and tell me what's so awful about having dinner with your father. We'll sit in my car.' He led her, protesting, towards it.

When they were seated in the shadowy darkness he reached for a box of Kleenex. 'Here, blow your nose,' he ordered. 'If you really don't want to talk about it, that's okay. I don't wish to pry.'

She took a man-sized tissue, had a good blow and made an effort at self-control. She felt a complete idiot, going to pieces like that. And because he was obviously trying to be helpful it made her want to cry again. She drew a long, steadying breath and bit her trembling lips.

'So you had an argument with your father? Well, that's not so terrible,' he went on. 'Most people fall out with their parents at some time or other.'

Joanna sniffed and dabbed her nose again. 'N-no, we didn't quarrel,' she faltered, 'it was all perfectly civilized . . . on the surface. But, oh . . . he's absolutely impossible!' She found herself telling Giles about her father's unexpected arrival and the shock she'd had on meeting the new wife he had brought with him. 'She's about the same age as me, would you believe? I mean, he didn't warn me, and I was staggered. How *could* he? It sickens me.'

'You mean, because she's young enough to be his daughter? It's a fairly common occurrence, Joanna, men of a certain age chasing after their lost youth.'

'It's embarrassing—and ridiculous,' she said in disgust. 'Thank goodness I'm not likely to see very much of them, that's all.'

Giles stroked his long nose, his expression thoughtful. 'Perhaps you're a bit jealous of her?'

How *could* he be so reasonable and impartial? How *dared* he see both sides of the question when she felt betrayed. 'So what if I am? Don't I have a right to be?' she said rebelliously. 'All I ever wanted was normal parents, like everybody else. There's my mother on her third husband . . . '

He curbed a wry smile. 'Parents aren't plaster saints, Joanna. They're fallible human beings like the rest of us. And, as far as I can see, they don't seem to have done too badly by you.'

'Oh, no, I always had a comfortable home. There was always someone to look after me, and I could have had anything I asked for, but I never felt really *important* to them.' She chewed her thumb nail. 'Because I'm the misfit, I suppose,' she mumbled. 'They were astonished when I wanted to nurse instead of going to RADA, or ballet school, or whatever . . . '

'Who said you were a misfit? You're a competent nurse, aren't you? Your chromosomes just got packaged in a slightly different way from theirs. You followed your own inclinations, and they let you. Isn't that something to be grateful for?'

Giles had a point, of course, although she was loath to admit it. She scowled at him and picked the tissue to pieces.

'You're making a mess of my car,' he pointed out. 'And I think your trouble is a large dose of self-pity.'

'Oh, you do, do you? Well, it's fine for you to talk. You're not in my shoes, are you?' Joanna snapped.

There was a long pause while he eyed her mutinous expression. Then he went on: 'Well, what can't be cured must be endured, so why don't you snap out of it and accept the situation? It can work out quite well, you know, older men and younger women. Much better than the other way around, in fact.'

He was so infuriatingly logical, she could have thumped him; sitting there being wise and not even sympathising with her, the rat. She let fly: 'Oh, for goodness' sake . . . don't preach at me! You sound like a Victorian patriarch.'

'And you wouldn't have liked one of those for a father, would you?'

She nibbled at another of her fingernails, but then she couldn't help a rueful smile. 'No, I certainly wouldn't.'

'You see. It's that headstrong streak of yours. But I expect it's all written in your stars,' he teased. Pulling her hand away from her mouth, he inspected the bitten nail and tutted.

'Yes, I'm a hopeless case, aren't I?' Joanna admitted. 'Well, if you've finished dishing out the good advice, and psychoanalysing me, perhaps I could go home? I shan't throw myself in the river, or anything.'

'Good. That's one casualty I've spared the A & E boys.' Giles started up the car and drove her the short distance to the Nurses' Home. 'And this concert of your father's . . . will you go?' he asked, pulling up outside.

She wrinkled her nose. 'No, I don't think so.'

'You should, you know. He probably wants your approval.'

She stared at him through slightly moist lashes. 'Do you really think that?'

'Yes, we all like to be approved of, don't we?'

'Well, I don't know . . . ' It wasn't a situation she relished. 'I wouldn't like to go on my own, and I don't feel like telling anyone else yet . . . '

'I'll come, if you like. Would that help?' Giles offered unexpectedly.

Joanna's blue eyes widened. 'That's awfully nice of you, but there's no reason for you to get

involved in my problems. I wasn't fishing . . . '
she hastened to add.

'I didn't suppose you were. So that's settled,
then,' he concluded briskly. 'You can give me the
details later. Goodnight, and pleasant dreams. And
don't worry about your father . . . he's old
enough to look after himself.'

She caught the faint male scent of his skin as he
leaned across to open the car door for her. Her
earlier resentment had subsided and in its place
was a curious mixture of feelings; gratitude for his
concern mingled with a pleasurable excitement that
caused a flutter in her throat. As usual in moments
of emotion, she was lost for words. And on impulse
she did what came naturally. 'Goodnight . . .
and thanks,' she said, and kissed him quickly
before leaving the car.

It was only afterwards, when she was in bed and
mulling over the events of the evening, that it
struck her how presumptuous she had been. Good
heavens! Staff nurses didn't go kissing senior
surgeons without encouragement. And even if he
hadn't thought at first that she was fishing, that
kiss might have changed his mind!

Why did it have to be *him* she'd bumped into
on the way home? Joanna agonized. As if she
hadn't enough on her plate without stepping out
of line at the hospital! But what the heck—Giles
was only a man, after all, she reminded herself. He
was not a god. At work he did his job the same as
she did hers. Oh well, she would just have to find
some way of explaining that he'd caught her off
balance tonight.

Sister Judd, handing over to Joanna at lunchtime next day, told her that a patient for partial-thyro-idectomy had been admitted that morning. 'She's a GP admission—Mrs Hazel Wing, twenty-four years old. She's rather keyed up about the whole thing, but she's not having surgery until Thursday, which gives us time to calm her down. Be sure to tell the night staff we want a sleeping pulse at two a.m. I've put her in with Lucy as they're both young. They'll be company for each other.'

When the Sister had gone Joanna went to make herself known to the new patient. 'Hallo, Mrs Wing,' she said pleasantly. 'Settled in all right, have you?'

Hazel Wing would have been an attractive young woman had it not been for her staring eyes and over-anxious expression. Her voice was husky and her breathing rather laboured. 'Yes, thank you, Nurse. Oh dear!' she gave a nervous laugh, 'I wish it was over and done with. They're not going to do it for a couple of days. I don't know why I couldn't have stayed at home till then.'

'Well, there are a few checks to be done first, which are much easier if you're on the spot. And you'll be able to take it easy for a couple of days. Everything all right at home?'

'Oh yes, there's only my husband . . . and he can look after himself.'

'Fine!' Joanna smiled. 'You're Dr Cassidy's patient, aren't you?'

'Yes, do you know him?'

'Quite well . . . he's okay, isn't he?'

'Yes, he's really kind. And so was the other

doctor who came to see me at home. I thought
that was very good of him.'

'There you are then—you've nothing to worry
about,' Joanna assured her. 'You'll feel a new
woman when it's all over.' She looked across at
Lucy who had just returned from a visit to the
bathroom. 'And you've got a very nice room-mate
to keep you company,' she added, smiling.

Lucy raised a smile in return. 'Hallo . . . did
you have good days off?'

'Yes, great, thanks. It goes all too quickly,
though. I suppose you'll be going home soon now,
won't you?'

'Yes, I suppose so,' Lucy said reluctantly. 'I've
had my stitches out.'

She didn't seem particularly overjoyed at the
prospect, but that was not altogether surprising.
Going out to pick up the reins of her old life would
be bound to bring home the stark reality of her
boy-friend's death.

Joanna understood, but there was nothing she
could do to make it less painful. After a few more
friendly words with them both, she left the two
patients talking together.

During visiting time that afternoon she took the
opportunity to explain to two of the student nurses
the nature of Hazel Wing's illness, and how essential it was to be reassuring when dealing with
thyrotoxic patients.

'There's been a considerable strain on her heart
and nervous system, so we need to keep her calm
and unworried to avoid the risk of surgical complications.'

'I did her obs when she was admitted, and her

hands were awfully sweaty,' said Carol. 'She was quite embarrassed about it. Will that go, after the operation?'

'It should do; they won't remove all the gland, just enough to correct her basal metabolism,' Joanna explained. After going a little more fully into the functions of the thyroid gland to make sure they understood what was involved, she sent the two students to tea.

She was checking the list of tests that were yet to be done when Shaun Cassidy bowled into the office.

'The saints be praised!' he exclaimed blithely, 'I hoped I'd find you here—and here you are. Pre-ordained it must have been, our meeting on Sunday like that.'

Joanna rolled her eyes to heaven, but she grinned. 'Whatever made you decide to park yourself down this way?'

'Fate, my love. And is that the way to be greeting an old friend?'

Now that she was over the first shock, oddly, seeing him again wasn't as difficult as she thought it might be. Probably because she didn't care any more. And lots of people had affairs that fizzled out, didn't they? You just put it down to experience.

'Well, to what do we owe this visit? You didn't just come to see me, did you?' she asked.

'Not entirely. Has my Mrs Wing arrived?'

Joanna nodded. 'Yes. Now *there's* a person who thinks you're a nice guy, strangely enough. Do you want to see her?'

'Yes, please. I shall come back and talk to *you*

later,' he chided, and chucked her under the chin.

She took him to the bedside and left him with his patient. He returned after some ten minutes and pronounced himself well pleased with Mrs Wing's state of mind. 'She seems fairly resigned and not too het up. I had wondered if she'd chicken out at the last minute.'

'You must have worked the old Irish charm on her,' Joanna said.

He perched on a corner of the desk and regarded her thoughtfully for a time. Then he startled her by saying, apparently in all seriousness, 'Jo . . . a GP needs a wife. Will you marry me?'

She was momentarily dumbstruck. All the while they had been dating he had never mentioned marriage. She swallowed, then laughed. 'Sorry, Shaun, but I don't need a husband.'

'Oh, come on, sweetheart. We were good together, weren't we?'

'So you were with quite a few other girls,' Joanna reminded him.

'I'm a reformed character, I promise you,' he cajoled, devilment in his dark eyes.

She shook her head. 'Let's settle for friendship. I like you, but I don't love you. And I do have some work to do, if you don't mind.'

'All right, we'll leave it there for now, but I shall ask you again, in more propitious circumstances. I'll be around. I'm going to be doing my turn one day a week in your Casualty Department.' Shaun departed, as jaunty as ever and not in the least abashed by her refusal.

Watching him go, Joanna shook her head indulgently. Doubtless some girl would fall for his blarney before too long. But not her any more. She made a couple of telephone calls and then went for her own tea when the other girls came back.

Upon her return she found that in her absence the hospital doctors had arrived to examine Hazel Wing.

'It's Mr Beltane and Steve. Eunice is with them,' Carol told her. 'Do you want me to do the four-hourlies?'

'Yes, fine. And after that you could start getting people up for supper.'

Joanna decided to leave Eunice chaperoning the doctors while she got on with changing a couple of dressings which needed to be done. She felt a little nervous about seeing Giles after last night. She wondered if, in the light of day, he'd had second thoughts about his offer to take her to her father's concert. Well, if he had he could always plead pressure of work, couldn't he? All the same, even chatting to the patients and concentrating on their dressings with her usual care failed to stop her heart stampeding. Having finished her work she was washing her hands before starting on the drugs round when the doctors emerged from seeing Mrs Wing.

Steve went off with Eunice to get some specimen phials for a blood test. Giles joined Joanna at the sink preparatory to washing his own hands.

'And how are you this afternoon?' he enquired casually.

'Fine, thanks,' she returned calmly, in spite of the turmoil in her chest. She dried her hands on a paper towel and watched him meticulously wash his own. 'Giles,' she hesitated, operating the waste container with her foot and holding it there for him to dispose of his own used towel, 'about last night . . . shall we forget what we arranged . . . about you coming to my father's concert?'

'Why?' He subjected her to a long straight look from beneath his dark brows. 'Have you decided not to go?'

'No, but I really shouldn't have let you in for it. I don't know why I did.'

'Another one of your spur of the moment reactions?' he suggested. 'Like your impulsive kiss?'

Reminded of that, her cheeks went hot and she laughed self-consciously. 'Yes, something like that. I mean, I had no right to involve you in my problems.'

He rolled down his shirt sleeves and fastened the cuffs before flashing her another questioning glance. 'If I remember rightly, I involved myself. Would this change of heart have anything to do with your friend Dr Cassidy?'

'No. Why do you ask that?'

'I just wondered. We met downstairs and he told me he'd seen you. I thought perhaps you'd decided you'd prefer the company of an old friend.'

'No, it wasn't that at all. I-I hadn't seen Shaun for months . . . and I'm not a man-chaser,' she added, on her dignity.

A smile flickered in his shrewd eyes. 'That being the case, I shan't be in danger of misconstruing your motives, shall I? We'll leave things as they stand. As a matter of fact I'm quite looking forward to an evening of music. It's some time since I had a purely social night out. Now, shall we get down to business? I want to have a chat about Mrs Wing.'

They went back to the office together and Giles outlined the procedure he wished followed to prepare the patient for her operation.

'She's to have an ECG and a chest X-ray,' he said, writing out the forms. 'I've explained to her that I shall make the cut in the natural fold of her neck so that the scar will hardly show, and I've assured her that her voice won't be affected. I've told her she'll be able to eat and drink normally in a few days and I hope I've put her mind at ease. Dorian will be up tomorrow to check her out. Okay? And we'll have a couple of packs of blood on standby, in case of emergency.' He rose to go. 'If I don't see you tomorrow, what time shall I pick you up?'

'Well, the concert begins at eight. So I should think . . . about seven-thirty?'

He nodded. 'Seven-thirty it is. Don't be late!' and he walked away.

She was left with a curious sense of forces beyond her control; that beneath the normality of a simple visit to a concert, far-reaching influences were at work. There was no doubt that his physical presence would be a comfort in what might not be the easiest of situations. On the other hand, that same physical presence produced a flurry of feelings within her that were far from comforting. It was clear that for his part he was merely being obliging. And that's the attitude she would have to adopt, if she wanted to preserve her sanity. She simply must not lose her head over another handsome charmer.

Resolutely Joanna pushed personal matters to the back of her mind and concentrated on her work.

The following day was a busy one with other admissions to be prepared for surgery. Dorian came up to check that the new patients were fit for anaesthesia and to get consent forms signed. Mrs Wing's chest X-ray and ECG had been satisfactory and she was relieved to hear that she was to be first on the list.

'You'll get a sedative tonight,' Joanna told her, 'and in the morning you'll be getting your pre-med. One of the nurses from the ward will go down with you, and by the time I come on duty at one o'clock tomorrow you'll be back here in the ward and it will all be over.'

Mrs Wing drew a long, nervous breath. 'Oh gosh, I wish it was this time tomorrow.'

'Is your husband coming to see you tonight?' Joanna asked.

'Yes, he said he would.'

'That will pass the time then, won't it? Try not to worry, Hazel,' she comforted. 'By next week you'll be amazed how well you feel.'

Leaving the ward at four-thirty that afternoon Joanna could also have wished that it were this time tomorrow. She wished with all her heart that she hadn't mentioned the wretched concert to Giles. Now she was committed to going, or have him think she was a petulant brat. And somehow, although she had no wish to seek his company, his good opinion mattered to her.

It had been a cool, cloudy day and a faint drizzle had set in. Looking up at the grey sky as she left the hospital, Joanna hugged her cloak around her. The weather exactly matched her mood. Coming off duty at the same time, Gail caught up with her and they hurried back to the Nurses' Home together.

'Dorian asked me for drinks in the mess tonight. Coming?' Gail said.

Joanna explained why not. Since meeting her father she'd hardly seen Gail, and she hadn't mentioned her brush with Giles in the car-park. Now she explained: 'I was telling GB about my dad's concert. He said he'd like to come, so he's picking me up here at half-seven.'

'Oh! He is, is he?' Gail remarked, archly. 'What have you got that the rest of us haven't?'

'A father who plays in a band,' laughed Joanna. 'Giles thinks a spot of music will improve his theatre technique tomorrow.'

'Well, that's a new line if ever I heard one! If he's full of the joys tomorrow then, we shall know why.'

The rain had come on in earnest when it was time for Joanna to leave. She had dressed in a cream linen suit with an emerald green blouse underneath, and she wore the emerald ear-rings that her mother had brought back from one of her trips abroad. She was ready and waiting in the lobby when Giles drew up in the road outside.

Pausing to put up her umbrella, she made a dash to where he was parked, and he pushed open the door for her.

'Thanks,' she said, putting the umbrella down by her feet as she settled in beside him. 'Sorry to drag you out on such an awful night.'

'The weather won't matter once we get there,' he returned, driving smoothly away. 'What nicer way to spend a wet evening?'

Being so close to him in the confined atmosphere was having its customary effect on her equilibrium. As always his physical presence set all her nerves alight. His classic dark head sitting squarely on his straight shoulders, overwhelmingly masculine, seduced her senses. And all this combined with the purpose of their journey heightened her tension.

'The Regency Centre, isn't it?' Giles's deep voice broke in on her thoughts. 'Do we have tickets?'

'No . . . my father said he'd leave them at the box office for me.'

'I saw a poster somewhere . . . the Franklin Jazz Band . . . is that right?'

'Yes. My father plays clarinet, amongst other things. How about you?' she asked by way of conversation. 'Do you play anything?'

He gave a slight smile. 'I owned a guitar in my youth, but I wouldn't say I hit the headlines. However, I appreciate good music.'

Drawing up outside the Centre, he went on, 'I'll drop you here and you can be picking up your tickets while I park the car.'

'Okay, thanks.' She didn't bother with the umbrella as she ran the few yards through the rain to the foyer of the theatre. It was milling with people. She joined the queue for tickets, but on reaching the pay desk she found there had been none put aside in the name of Leigh. That didn't surprise Joanna in the least. It would have been more surprising if her father had remembered.

Fortunately seats were available so she bought two for the stalls and was rather glad that Giles had not been with her. It would have seemed even more of a liberty on her part if he'd paid for the tickets, which he might have insisted on doing.

Presently she spotted his arrival and went to join him.

'Got the tickets, have we? Fine,' he said. 'No time for a drink, I'm afraid. We'll get one in the interval,' and they made their way towards the auditorium. 'The last time I came here,' he volunteered when they were settled in their seats, 'was a Christmas carol concert many moons ago when I was a student.'

'A medical student?' she queried.

'Yes. Before that my recollections are lost in cobwebs.'

'Oh, come on,' she returned lightly, 'you're not that ancient.'

'I feel it sometimes. There's a certain person puts years on me,' he added, casting her a wry, meaningful look.

'Really? I thought you were impregnable,' she murmured, and concentrated on studying the programme.

They discussed the various items together. It was a fairly conservative selection, catering for popular taste, and there were two solo spots for the singer, billed as Kay Sinclair, with numbers from hit musicals.

From behind the safety curtain they could hear small flurries of notes as the players completed their tuning up. Then the auditorium lights dimmed, there was an expectant hush, and the curtain rose.

The performance began with a spirited rendering of music from *West Side Story*.

Smartly turned out in dark blue silver-trimmed monkey-jackets, the two dozen bandsmen were grouped in a semi-circle around their conductor. Their music stands carried matching blue satin banners with silver logos. And they played with all the panache and polish associated with American big bands.

'Which one is your father?' Giles wanted to know, his foot tapping to the music.

'Third from the right. He's playing saxophone at the moment.' She thought how very distinguished he looked, and felt rather proud of his expertise. 'I've never actually been to one of their concerts before,' she whispered. 'Rather good, aren't they?'

Giles nodded. 'It must be very satisfying to get to that degree of excellence.'

'Yes, I suppose so. But it's a precarious sort of life.'

'That applies to life in general these days,' he returned. 'You have to accept the risks and do what you're best at.'

They settled back to enjoy familiar tunes by Irving Berlin and stirring marches by Sousa. The last item before the interval was one of the vocal numbers. Kay came onto the stage stunningly dressed in a slinky white glittery gown, her auburn hair in tumbled waves about her bare shoulders.

'That's my new stepmother,' Joanna said.

Giles raised his eyebrows appreciatively. 'Your father has taste. Let's hope she sounds as good as she looks.'

They were not disappointed. The girl had a pleasing soprano voice and an attractive manner. She sang songs from *Porgy and Bess,* scaling the high notes effortlessly and earning well-deserved applause.

'Funny how my father seems to fall for singers,' Joanna said, sipping a glass of white wine during the interval.

'Why . . . was your mother a singer?'

'No, she's a violinist. But it was another singer he walked out on us for.'

A few subtle promptings from Giles had her revealing quite a lot about her unconventional family. 'So this is what produced your bundle of insecurities?' he teased.

Joanna laughed. 'Is that what you think? I'm really quite happy with my lot, even if I am the maverick. I prefer my way of life to theirs.'

The music had already worked its magic on her mood and by the time the final item was played she felt in good heart. 'I really enjoyed that,' she said with a wide smile at her companion. 'Did you?'

'Yes, I did,' Giles nodded. 'And now . . . you're going backstage to see him, are you?'

'I suppose I ought.' She wrinkled her nose. 'Are you coming too?'

'No, you'd better do that bit on your own. I'll collect my raincoat from the cloakroom and wait for you out front.'

'Okay. I won't be long.'

In the gangway they parted company. She went in the direction of the stage and through one of the small side doors. There was considerable activity going on behind the scenes with players packing up their instruments and equipment. Some were already departing through the exit door to where their coach waited in a side street.

Joanna approached a man with a large leather trumpet case under his arm. 'Excuse me . . . is Ed Leigh still around?'

'I couldn't say, honey. He'll be up there if he is,' and he jerked his head towards the small flight of steps leading to the stage before going on his way.

She paused as another bandsman came down the stairs, and she repeated her question.

'Sure, baby.' He ran a practised eye over her neat curves. 'Go on up. Hey, Ed!' he called back, 'there's a lady here asking for you. Some guys have all the luck!' His cheeky wolf-whistle followed her as she ran up the steps.

She found her father chatting with the drummer while they packed up their kit. His mouth fell open in surprise when he saw her. 'Jo-jo! I never expected to see you.'

'You invited me, didn't you?' she smiled.

'So I did, but I didn't think . . . ' His hand flew to his mouth, 'and I forgot the tickets. I'm the pits, aren't I?' He seized her in his arms and gave her a bear-hug. 'Anyway, you came. Isn't that nice! Chuck,' he turned to the drummer, 'meet my lovely daughter. She's a nurse. She's the only useful member of the family. We're very proud of her.'

'I don't know about that,' Joanna laughed. 'Your music tonight was really great. And Kay has a gorgeous voice.'

'Yes, she's ace, isn't she?' he beamed. 'Come on back to the hotel with us for a drink. We can squeeze you into the coach if you haven't got transport.'

'Well, thanks all the same, Dad, but there's someone waiting for me, and I don't think he'd want to make a night of it. He's operating tomorrow.'

'Oh, Mr Right?' he asked, eyebrows raised. 'Fix it up in the next three weeks and I could give you away.'

'No, not Mr Right,' Joanna grinned. 'I'm steering clear of the matrimonial hang-ups for the time being.'

He made a wry face. 'Yeah, I'm not much of an example, am I? Still, this time it's for keeps. You'll see.'

The drummer said he was glad to have met her and lumbered out with his equipment. Joanna and her father stood talking for a while longer until someone yelled that the coach was ready to leave and what the hell was keeping Ed.

They went down the stairs together and out of the side door. Joanna waved to Kay and tossed a kiss through the rain-spattered coach window, then she kissed her father fondly goodbye. 'I really do hope you'll both be happy,' she said.

'Bless you. And give my best to your mother when you see her. I'm thrilled that you came tonight. Keep in touch, Jo-jo.'

She felt on top of the world as she ran round to the front of the building to where Giles sat waiting in the car. Her face was wet with rain and she helped herself to one of his tissues to mop up. 'It's all right,' she said, a little breathless after her dash, 'I'm not crying.'

'I'm relieved to hear it,' he said. 'All plain sailing?'

'Yes, he was really pleased I showed up, although he didn't expect me,' she smiled. 'We were invited back to their hotel for drinks, but I thought you'd probably rather not.'

'So you deprived me of a nightcap, did you?' Giles said in mock dismay.

'Oh, be honest. You wouldn't have wanted to go. I'll make you a cup of coffee if you want a nightcap,' she returned cheerfully.

'Are you allowed to entertain men in your rooms?'

'Of course. This *is* the twentieth century, you know.'

He gave a half-smile. 'Perhaps I could take you up on that when you move into your new house. I'll settle for one of your impulsive gestures tonight.'

'If it's pre-ordered it could hardly be called impulsive,' she contradicted, an odd feeling in the pit of her stomach.

'No, I suppose not.'

They lapsed into silence until they reached the Nurses' Home.

'Thanks again for coming,' Joanna said, and wondered if she ought, or ought not to offer him the gesture he'd referred to.

She could tell by the devilment in his eyes that he could read her mind. He settled the matter by taking her hand and kissing it. 'Off to bed with you,' he said dismissively.

CHAPTER SIX

JOANNA did a great deal of serious thinking after leaving Giles. There was no doubt he had been right in advising her to support her father. She was glad now that she had made the effort; his obvious pleasure on seeing her had been worth that. All the same, it rankled to have been put straight by the surgeon.

Uncanny how that man had the power to disturb her, both mentally and physically. She wondered if he were aware of the sensual excitement she felt whenever they were in close proximity? She did her best not to let it show, but you could do little about those mysterious laws of attraction that operated of their own free will.

It was something she was going to have to play down, because she had no intention of letting her bodily antenna get the upper hand. And he certainly showed no signs in that direction. To him she was just a pain in the neck who constantly got in his way. In any case, the man constantly ruffled her feathers, didn't he? He was always so exasperatingly right! No, Mr Giles Beltane, I refuse to lose my head over you, she told herself.

Dressing to go on duty at one o'clock the following day, Joanna found the surgeon still uppermost in her thoughts. She pictured him in his theatre gear. At this hour he would already have put in a good morning's work. By all accounts, provided nobody did anything utterly stupid, his operating sessions flowed with the minimum of fuss and maximum efficiency.

Hazel Wing's thyroidectomy would by now be well on the way to completion . . . and that would be one very happy lady when it was all over. Correction of an over-active thyroid gave results which seemed miraculous to the patient and were equally rewarding to the surgeon. There must be tremendous satisfaction in being able to change people's lives for the better, Joanna reflected. On the other hand, it was an ironic twist of fate that a man like Giles had been able to do nothing to save his own wife. Things like that were a grim reminder of human limitations.

The rain had ceased overnight and a fragrant June day greeted Joanna as she stepped out in good spirits towards the hospital with just a navy cardigan over her blue uniform dress. On her way through the lobby she picked up her post; a letter from her old flatmate in London and postcards from Brussels and Hamburg from her mother. These she read while eating her sandwich lunch in the canteen before going up to the ward.

There was a faint whiff of food throughout the hospital corridors with the remains of patients' lunches stacked on trolleys waiting to be collected. Joanna paused to hold open the door of Paget Ward as the domestic backed her way through carrying the large communal teapot.

'Thanks, ducks,' Agnes said. She jerked her head towards the office where Sister Judd, her brow furrowed, was giving instructions to two of the staff. 'Don't know what's 'appened, but she seems to be in a right mood over something. Fair snapped my 'ead off because I dropped a plate on the floor.'

On operating days there was always a certain amount of tension on the ward with the extra work involved. As well as the normal routine tasks to be done, there were the patients to be got ready for surgery, the right documents sent to theatre with them, and their beds to be remade to await their return. After that came the need for careful monitoring until they were properly round from the anaesthetic.

It was unusual for Sister Judd to get rattled. Normally she took it all in her stride, but today she was obviously upset about something.

'Put her things in a plastic bag and strip the bed,' Joanna heard her say, ' . . . and if Lucy asks questions you can tell her that Mrs Wing will be going to another ward.'

Beryl gave Joanna a plaintive look in passing.

'Good afternoon, Sister,' Joanna said, puzzled. 'What's going on?'

'Mrs Wing arrested in theatre,' the Sister returned quietly.

Joanna's mouth dropped open in dismay. 'Oh, no! Is she . . . ?'

The Sister shrugged. 'Can't say yet . . . they're working on her. Poor Mr Beltane . . . it's every surgeon's nightmare.'

'Poor Hazel!' Joanna felt stunned. 'And we were telling her how wonderful she was going to feel. Oh dear! Was it on the table? How far had they got?'

'I think it must've been in the recovery room. They'd already rung through to say Miss Janes could have her pre-med, then they rang back to say hold it, there was a crisis—but we'd already given it.' Sister Judd let out a heartfelt sigh and shook her head despairingly. 'Let's hope there'll be some better news before her husband rings.' Resolutely she squared her solid shoulders. 'Well, the work must go on. You do the drugs, will you? I'll go for my lunch now and I'll see what I can find out. In any case, whatever happens she won't be coming back here today.'

Joanna collected Carol to help her with the medicines. They both felt desperately sorry, but they had to keep their knowledge to themselves and carry on as normal.

'All right, Miss Janes?' Joanna switched on a cheerful expression, looking behind the drawn bed-curtains where the middle-aged schoolmistress lay ready gowned for her operation.

'Yes, dear.' The patient was still alert despite her pre-medication. 'When will they be coming for me?'

'Shouldn't be long now. They got held up a bit downstairs,' Joanna said tactfully. 'Don't you feel sleepy yet?'

'Not really,' Miss Janes replied. 'Just pleasantly lazy, and my mouth's rather dry. I don't feel at all apprehensive though.'

'Well, there's nothing to worry about, is there? Vein stripping isn't a perilous operation. Try shutting your eyes and thinking nice thoughts. You'll probably drop off before you know it.' With a smile Joanna closed the curtains again.

When Sister Judd returned from lunch she brought the hopeful news that Hazel Wing had been resuscitated and was now in Intensive Care.

'The thyroidectomy was a complete success—there was no malignancy. She went into heart block as they were about to take her to the recovery room. Anyway, they've managed to get her going again. Now we shall have to wait and see how she does.'

The rest of the scheduled list of operations got under way. By four o'clock Miss Janes was back in the ward with her legs bandaged from groin to toes, and their last patient—Mr Hardwick for herniotomy—was on his way to the anaesthetics room.

Sister Judd prepared to hand over before going off duty. 'Well, it should all be plain sailing now, Joanna. Lucy's mother will be here to collect her shortly. I've got her medical certificate signed but there's still her outpatient appointment to be arranged. Get on to that, will you?'

'Okay, Sister, I'll do it now.' Joanna lifted the telephone and rang the appointments desk. She made the necessary arrangement, filled out a card and took it to the girl who was already dressed and waiting to be called for. 'Here you are, Lucy. Mr Beltane will see you in Outpatients in two weeks' time. Come up and see us afterwards, won't you? We're going to miss you.'

'I'll miss you, too. You've all been terrific.' Lucy's eyes were suspiciously bright.

Joanna put her arm around the girl and gave her a hug. 'It's not going to be easy for you at first, I know,' she sympathised, 'but it will get better. Don't avoid people, will you? Get out and meet your friends, and talk about Tony if you want to. It's much the best way.'

'I'll try,' Lucy said, 'but everyone's not as easy to talk to as you are. I wish . . . ' she paused, looking wistful, then apparently thought better of what she was about to say. 'Pity I can't say goodbye to Hazel. Remember me to her and say I hope she gets on all right.'

'I will,' Joanna said, 'and you take good care of yourself.'

The rest of the day ran smoothly with no more scares. Mr Hardwick arrived back from theatre with his hernia successfully repaired, and Miss Janes was washed, put back into her own nightdress and given the prescribed post-operative analgesic. All was calm and peaceful by the time the doctors came to the ward late that evening to check on their cases.

Giles was accompanied by his registrar, Peter Green, and houseman Steve. They were a pretty solemn trio as they went around assuring themselves that all was well with their other patients. Joanna returned with them to the office where Giles paused to confer on one or two points. Up until then no one had made any reference to the arrest in theatre.

Joanna looked anxiously from one to the other. 'How is Mrs Wing?' she asked.

'Holding her own, I hope,' Giles said, sombrely.

Peter wiped imaginary sweat from his brow. 'Phew! First time that's happened to me in theatre. I nearly had a baby!'

'*You* did! The buck stops here,' returned Giles. 'I'm going along to ICU now to see how she is. I'll let you know if there's any change.'

He stalked off, hands in his pockets and a weariness about him that made Joanna long to be of some comfort. She sighed. 'Poor Giles . . . it's a tremendous responsibility. And you both look knackered. Want a coffee?'

'Has anyone ever told you you're an angel?' Steve said.

She laughed. 'Not lately,' and she went to make the drinks while the doctors got down to their writing.

It was nine p.m. and Joanna was giving her handover report to the night staff before Giles returned. She looked up expectantly. 'Carry on,' he said, 'I'll be with you in a minute,' and went into the ward to look at another of his patients.

He joined her when she was ready to leave the ward. 'Well, how is she?' Joanna asked.

He held up his crossed fingers. 'So far, so good.' They walked down the stairs together. 'I think she's going to make it. I've been having a chat with her husband. Dr Cassidy had warned him that her heart was under strain. All the same, he's pretty shattered, poor guy.' He ran a hand through his dark hair. 'I sometimes wish I'd gone in for market gardening, or house painting, or road mending—anything but messing with other people's lives.'

'Oh, come on,' Joanna said, 'don't talk daft. If it hadn't been you it would have been somebody else. And someone's got to patch people up. Now who's wallowing in self-pity?'

'I suppose I walked right into that one.' He gave a short laugh. 'Well, since you feel qualified to dish out the pearls of wisdom this time, I think you should spend the rest of the evening cheering me up.'

Going out into the cool night air, Joanna knotted the sleeves of her cardigan around her shoulders. 'Me cheer you up?' she challenged jokingly, 'I always thought I had the opposite effect.'

'You're a counter-irritant,' he told her.

'Thanks very much! And you're a real grouch tonight. Go home and take a dose of liver salts.'

'Then you'd best come with me and see that I do,' Giles said.

Joanna giggled. 'Now you really are being ridiculous.'

They had arrived at the car-park and he paused by his car. 'Well, you owe me a favour,' he growled. 'Come on,' he opened the door of the passenger seat, 'I can't face eating alone tonight.'

She glanced down at her uniform doubtfully. 'Okay . . . but can't I go home and change first?'

'What does it matter what you look like? We'll eat at my place. The only audience you'll have is me.' He hustled her inside and shut the door.

This is absolutely crazy, she thought. How did I get into this? She pulled the clips from her cap, tossed it behind her and combed through her fair hair with her fingers.

He certainly was in a downbeat mood. Joanna stole discreet glances at his mournful expression. Heaviness sat on him like a cloak and she could think of nothing to say to lift him out of it.

'How's your father?' she thought to ask.

Giles broke out of his broody meditations. 'My

father? Oh, he's fine. He's convalescing at his holiday home in Jersey.'

'Oh, I'm so glad. Will he retire, do you think?'

'Not altogether . . . but he'll probably slow up a bit.'

Well, at least there was no problem there. It must be just Mrs Wing's condition which was preying on his mind. It was always more poignant when the lives of young people were threatened, and she could understand his despondency. Anyway, she had got him off the subject, which was something. As a counter-irritant she might be quite remedial, Joanna decided with a private smile.

He had driven through the town and out to a spacious block of luxury flats fronting a broad stretch of the river. The upper apartments had wrought-iron balconies overlooking the promenade gardens.

Giles let her into his rooms on the second floor. His living-room was comfortably furnished with hide-covered easy chairs, a cinnamon carpet and floor-length velour drapes at the window.

He switched on wall-lights and a large table-lamp before tossing off his jacket and removing his tie. 'Make yourself at home,' he said. 'Would you like to have a wash?'

His close-fitting trousers hugged his powerful thighs, showing the potent strength of his lithe body. Joanna felt a melting sensation inside her, and tried not to look. 'I think I will,' she said.

In the bathroom she washed her face and hands, combed her hair, and felt very dowdy in her forget-me-not blue uniform dress. Even if she wanted—which she didn't—she was certainly not going to

arouse anyone's animal passions in *that* get-up!
She could hear Giles moving about in the kitchen
and went to find him tipping ice cubes into a basin.

'What will you have to drink?' he asked, looking
round when she appeared.

'Orange juice . . . or something soft, please.'
She intended to keep all her wits about her.

He took a carton from the fridge, poured juice
into a tumbler, topped it up with ice and handed
it to her. Then he swallowed a mouthful of his
own drink and went to inspect the contents of his
larder.

'Oh—there's not a lot. My daily replenishes me
tomorrow. Cheese, bacon, eggs, or something out
of a tin. What do you fancy?'

'How about an omelette?' Joanna suggested.

He made a comic face. 'My cooking skills don't
extend that far.'

She smiled. 'I'll do it—they're my pièce de résist-
ance. Grill me some bacon and find me a basin
and things.'

Raising his eyebrows, he took another drink,
then set about producing what she asked for.
'Bossy little thing, aren't you?' He watched her
whisk the mixture and butter the pan.

'My Aunt Beth always says a good meal is the
best tonic for a bout of the blues,' she returned,
determinedly cheerful. She passed him the kitchen
scissors. 'Is that bacon ready? Chop it up for me,
would you.'

'Who's Aunt Beth?' he wanted to know, meekly
doing what she asked.

Joanna chattered away while she cooked, keeping
her eyes on her job and ignoring the flutters in her

stomach whenever their bodies brushed in passing. 'She's not really my aunt—she started off as our nanny and stayed on. She's always seemed like family. We're all very fond of her.'

She turned the food on to plates, and they ate her melting, golden concoctions at his breakfast bar. 'So this is what an omelette should taste like,' Giles remarked. 'I always thought they were made of rubber.'

'My one claim to artistry,' she boasted. 'I always make the omelettes when I'm home.'

He had mellowed considerably by now. 'If you'd like to put your feet up, I'll make the coffee.'

'You go and put *your* feet up,' Joanna returned. 'I'm the one who's giving the orders tonight.'

'Don't argue with me,' Giles said sternly. 'Do as you're told. And why don't you take off that ridiculous dress . . . it reminds me of the hospital.'

'Well, you wouldn't let me change. And I'm not going to do a strip-tease for your benefit,' she said rebelliously. 'Anyway, you said it didn't matter what I looked like.'

'All right—we'll scrub that.' He turned her by the shoulders and pushed her out of the kitchen. 'Go and sit down.'

She planted herself in one corner of the leather sofa, kicked off her shoes and put her feet up. He might have relaxed, but despite her determination to remain in control her tension had increased as the evening wore on. She knew she ought not to be sitting there tête-à-tête with him, considering the effect he had on her. As soon as they'd had the coffee she would ask to leave. It was after eleven in any case, and he did seem to have perked up.

Joanna stretched and breathed deeply in an effort to unwind. She occupied herself by taking stock of her surroundings. The wall opposite the window housed a large fitment containing a stereo, books, and the various impedimenta of modern living. In front of her was a rather nice watercolour of The Backs at Cambridge University, and poised above a teak writing-desk was a pair of rowing sculls and a photograph of a rowing eight.

Giles cut short her survey by coming in with the coffee. He put the two mugs on the long low table in front of the sofa, then crossed to the stereo, chose a cassette and slotted it in before coming to join Joanna. She would have moved her legs to make room, but he grasped her black-stockinged feet and rested them across his knee. 'That's all right—leave them there,' he said, patting them.

She could hardly do otherwise, not without an undignified tussle, since his large hand was imprisoning her ankles. But it wasn't exactly the right position to put her at ease.

Idly, he began to test her Babinski's reflex, running his thumb nail along the soles of her feet. He cast her a teasing glance. 'That seems fairly normal.'

Her pulse was racing, but she returned levelly: 'Well, I'm a fairly normal person.'

'Mmmm . . . and not a bad pair of fetlocks,' he went on, examining her ankles. Finally he tickled her toes.

She squirmed and managed to pull away, tucking her feet beneath her. 'Oh, for goodness' sake!' she laughed.

He restrained a grin and took up his coffee. She reached for hers, sat back and let the music soothe her rising qualms. It was unmistakable Chopin, familar and lyrical, although the name escaped her.

'Oh, this is nice,' she said, beginning to feel relaxed and dreamy and increasingly romantic. She finished her drink, sighed and went on, half-reluctantly, 'I really must be getting back. The counter-irritant seems to have done its work, anyway.'

'*I'll* be the judge of that.' Giles drew her firmly into the crook of his shoulder and patted her on the head. 'You be a good girl and stay put for a bit. No strings. Isn't this nice and cosy?'

It might very well be nice and cosy and no strings for him, but where did that leave her? Joanna's heart began to thud and it reached a crescendo when, presently, she felt his lips on her hair. Then, without any conscious effort on either part, or so it seemed, their mouths were together and her limbs felt weak with desire. His caresses were expert and seductive. Involuntarily her body moulded to his as his kiss deepened, sweeping away her defences. It was the texture of his skin rough against hers that finally brought her a degree of sanity.

She pulled away and said, shakily, 'Ouch! Your chin's like a scrubbing brush—you need a shave.'

He released his hold on her, stroked his jowl and gave a rakish grin. 'Would it be worth my while?'

'No, it wouldn't—don't push your luck,' she returned coolly, despite the storm inside her. 'That's enough tea and sympathy for one night. Time I went home.'

He rose and stretched like a big cat, his shoulder muscles rippling beneath the fine cotton of his white shirt. 'Okay, perhaps you're right this time. Get your things together, then.'

Giles replaced his tie and jacket. Joanna put on her shoes and smoothed her ruffled hair, wishing that her turbulent emotions could be as easily put to rights.

They drove through the summer night back towards the hospital. 'Thanks for coming,' he said, pulling up outside the Nurses' Home. 'I enjoyed your cooking . . . ' he restrained a smile, 'and your company.'

'Glad to be of service!' she quipped. 'It was nice for me too . . . it made a change from this place,' and she nodded towards the functional building.

He studied her intently for a long moment. 'Your eyes match the blue of your uniform.'

'Do they? Oh dear! And you think the uniform's yuk.'

'I don't object to the colour, but they're much too come-hither, so mind how you use them.'

He didn't attempt to kiss her goodnight, and she watched him drive on towards the hospital. Doubtless he would be checking up on Hazel Wing again, his mild flirtation with her already dismissed.

She ran up to her room gritting her teeth in annoyance and frustration. Well! He had a nerve, warning her against eye-talk! He should watch his own body-talk! What did he think she was made of . . . asbestos? That evening she had wanted to be of comfort to him, to help him over his depression. But that didn't entitle him to exploit the situation. Men—they were the end! They never missed a trick.

Gail, in her dressing-gown, was coming along the corridor from the bathroom, towel and toilet bag in her arms. She stared at Joanna in surprise. 'Where've you been at this time of night, and still in uniform?'

'Playing the good Samaritan. Giles hit a low after that business with Mrs Wing in theatre, so I went home with him and cooked him a meal to cheer him up.'

'You did *what?*'

Joanna laughed at her friend's incredulous expression. 'We-ell, we just happened to be leaving the ward at the same time, and we were talking about her, and I could see he was fed up . . . so I thought I'd do my bit to comfort the afflicted,' she joked.

Gail cocked an eyebrow and said, 'Hmmm!' with a wealth of meaning.

'It wasn't like that!' Joanna grinned. 'Anyway, I was feeling awful too, because I'd been telling Mrs Wing how great she was going to feel when it was all over. So it was kind of reciprocal.'

'Yes, well, it was pretty hairy at the time. Dorian was shattered as well, but it never occurred to me to cash in on it. You'll have to give me lessons.' Gail wanted to know where Giles lived and what his place was like. Presently, her curiosity satisfied, she changed the subject.

'By the way, I've heard from my cousin Pam. They're leaving for The Hague at the end of next week and we can move in on the Saturday. Well, she'd like us to as we've promised to look after the cat. That'll be all right, won't it?'

She followed Joanna into her room and sat on the bed to talk for a while. 'At last we shall be able to work up a decent social life for ourselves, shan't we, when we get anchored there.'

'Yes, great! I can't wait to leave this place,' Joanna agreed. 'It was really brill tonight, cooking in a decent kitchen and relaxing in a proper home.'

'And the rest!' cracked Gail, and took herself off to bed.

Joanna stepped out of her crumpled uniform, unpinned badges and emptied her pockets before dumping it in the laundry bag. Then she went to the bathroom and had a restorative soak in a scented bath.

Lying back letting the warm suds ease her tired muscles, she dwelt on her evening with Giles. She wondered whether he was thinking about it too? She hoped she had disturbed him as much as he had disturbed her. Serve him right if she had. Not that he had seemed at all bothered when she had called a halt to his love-making. He had treated the whole thing dismissively . . . as though it were just a tasty spin-off at the end of the meal. And since he had gone back to the hospital after leaving her, all he was likely to be concerned about was his patient.

Joanna sighed. Was she so forgettable? Damn the man! He had no right to go throwing rocks into her peaceful little pool.

CHAPTER SEVEN

BEFORE having her plans disrupted by Giles the previous night Joanna had been meaning to telephone Chelsea. It was Aunt Beth's birthday the following week. Since the rest of the family were away, Joanna thought she would dash up to town on her next day off, take Beth out to lunch and then perhaps go on to a show.

Up till now she'd had no time even to pass on the news about having seen her father. He had said he'd spoken to Beth, but Joanna wondered whether he had told her anything about his new bride. Tolerant though Beth was, she took a dim view of his chaotic love life, and he might well have avoided the subject.

Having taken ages to get to sleep Joanna awoke heavy-eyed the next morning. She felt hardly rested at all. Much as she had tried to put Giles out of her mind, thoughts of him stayed with her into the small hours. She swung between feeling annoyed by his casual attitude and disturbed by his power to arouse her. For one wild moment her body had thrilled to his touch and she could have thrown caution to the winds.

But if he thought she was going to be a handy lay when he happened to need one, Joanna brooded, he had better think again!

Even so, it might be difficult to resume normal relations after this. She wondered what his attitude would be when next they met? However, there was little point in worrying about it; she would face that problem when the time came.

After a wash and a reviving mug of coffee, Joanna armed herself with a supply of coins and went along in her dressing-gown to the communal pay phone in the corridor.

Beth was delighted to hear from her. 'Hello, my love! I've been meaning to ring you myself, only I never know the best time to catch you. Well, how's life?'

'Fine . . . it's all been happening here.' Joanna went on to tell her about the house she and Gail would be moving to: ' . . . and there's a double bed in my room, so you'll be able to come and stay if you ever feel like a weekend away.'

'Yes, that would nice. What a stroke of luck for you! By the way, did hear from your dad? He rang here and I gave him your number.'

'Yes, I did. We had dinner together. His band was playing at the Regency Centre near here—I went to the concert . . . it was great. He was just the same as ever, only older, of course. Beth, did he tell you he had married again?'

'Oh! No dear, he didn't. But it doesn't surprise me.' Beth gave a short laugh. 'Was she with him?'

'Yes . . . we met. She's very pretty, red-haired, although I expect it's tinted. She sings with the band. About twenty-five years younger than him, I would say.'

'Oh! And how did you feel about that?' Beth asked.

Joanna sighed. 'Well, not exactly ecstatic, but she seems nice enough. We all parted good friends.'

'No point in being otherwise,' the older woman said wisely. 'Life's too short for bearing grudges, isn't it?'

'Too true! Well, now we've got that out of the way, about your birthday. I'm coming up to town on Wednesday and I'd like to take you out to lunch. Then we could go on to a show, if I can get tickets. How about that?'

'Lovely! That's very sweet of you, Jo,' Beth said. 'I'll look forward to it. But . . . er . . . before we go any further, there's something I have to tell you . . . ' She paused, and a certain note in her voice started alarm bells ringing in Joanna's brain.

'Nothing wrong, is there?' she asked, concerned.

'Quite the reverse—at least from my point of view. Don't faint, but . . . I'm going to be married.'

Joanna caught her breath. '*What?* Did you say *married?*' she squeaked.

'Yes. It's a bit of a shock, I know,' Beth said. 'Sorry to spring it on you like this . . . '

'But . . . when did all this happen?' Joanna asked. 'Do I know him?'

'No, although I may have mentioned him from time to time. We met at the evening institute; you know, where I take the cookery classes. His name's John, and he's a widower. He came to the classes when he had to start cooking for himself. Well, it took off from there,' Beth rattled on. 'He's a chemist. He's just ten years older than me. We get on awfully well together . . . '

'Gosh!' Joanna exclaimed. 'You've taken my breath away. But that's terrific . . . I'm so glad. Do the others know?'

'Not yet. I knew he liked me, but the proposal took me by surprise, too. The thing is, Jo,' Beth confided, 'there's been talk lately about giving up this house. It's too big now that you're all leading your own lives. Your mother and Malcolm would prefer to move into a flat, but I know your mum was worried about what to do with me. Well, I mean, you don't really need me now. So this couldn't have happened at a better time for us all, could it?'

Joanna agreed, although she still found it difficult to take in. Sell the house in Chelsea? That would mean goodbye to her old room there, packing up or parting with the accumulation of years. The final severing of her roots.

'All the details when I see you, then,' Beth went on happily. They made plans as to where they would meet on the following Wednesday and said goodbye.

Going back to her room to get ready for work, Joanna was overwhelmed with nostalgia for the house she had known since childhood. True, wherever her mother moved, that would be home for Joanna, but as far back as she could remember Beth had always been part of it, dependable and reassuring. Now she wouldn't be any more. For the past twenty years though, she had been devoted to them all, so it was well-deserved that she should at last have found happiness for herself.

Joanna made an effort to come to terms with life's constantly-changing pattern. She would just have to put down roots of her own somewhere. Nothing stayed the same for ever, did it? Perhaps it was time she herself made another change. She could apply for a health visitors course . . . or maybe she might even follow up Kay's suggestion to try for a job in America.

For the moment though, there was the present to think about and duty called. But her thoughts were far away as she searched out a clean uniform, dressed and went over to the canteen to have her lunch.

She found Eunice and Beryl also there, talking about Paget Ward's latest emergency admission.

'This fellow tackled a couple of muggers who had picked on an old lady,' Eunice explained. 'He got knifed for his pains.'

'Oh, no! Much damage?' Joanna enquired.

'Almost severed his jugular and made a nice mess of his good looks,' Beryl said. 'I bet he'll think twice about going to the rescue in the future.'

Joanna pursed her lips. 'It's a spontaneous reaction, I expect. Although you can hardly blame people for not wanting to get involved.'

They finished their lunch and went up to the ward. Sister Judd was due to go off for her long weekend, and going through the Kardex with Joanna, she said:

'The new patient in the side ward is Richard Trent, twenty-two, a stabbing case . . . '

'Yes, I heard about him,' Joanna nodded. 'How is he?'

'Lucky to be alive. He lost a lot of blood,' Sister Judd told her. 'Still, they've done a good repair job on his face and neck. We need half-hourly observations until he's stable. Carol's been keeping an eye on him, but she should be relieved now to go to lunch. Give him the Pethidine when he needs it, and there's another pack of blood in the fridge when that one runs out.'

The Sister shook her head and tutted. 'Wretched thugs—they should be horsewhipped.' She passed over the ward keys. 'He's a student at the university. His relatives have been informed but they haven't visited yet—they've to come from Kent. Well, I'll be off now. You've got enough staff so you should be all right. 'Bye,' and she gathered up her belongings and left.

Joanna went first to the side ward opposite the office, where the student nurse was keeping watch over the new patient. 'You can go to lunch now, Carol,' she said. 'Everything okay?'

'Yes, I was just about to do his obs again.' The junior's face was full of pity. 'Poor bloke,' she murmured. 'Looks a mess, doesn't he?'

'Mmmm . . . not a pretty sight,' Joanna agreed, her eyes taking in the sorry state of the casualty. He lay on his uninjured side; a hefty young man with a shock of light brown hair. There was a dressing over his neck wound and his face was a mass of angry contusions amongst the black silk sutures. A blood transfusion dripped steadily into his forearm. 'All right, off you go,' she said. 'I'll do the necessary.'

Placing her fingers on the patient's wrist, Joanna consulted her fob-watch and timed his pulse rate, after which she checked his blood pressure. As she removed the cuff from his arm the young man stirred and muttered something unintelligible.

'Hallo, Richard,' she said in a gentle voice, bending over him, 'time to wake up. You're in bed in the ward now.'

His heavy lids fluttered and he looked at her with dazed brown eyes. 'I didn't die?' he mumbled.

She smiled at him. 'No, you didn't! There's lots more life in you yet. How's the pain?'

'Chronic. My head's splitting.'

'All right . . . I can give you something for that.'

'I feel sick,' he suddenly croaked, raising himself on one elbow.

She grabbed the bowl from his locker and held it for him while he retched. Afterwards he floppped back, trembling, clammy and exhausted. Joanna moistened a gauze swab with cold water and carefully sponged his face. 'You'll probably feel better after that,' she comforted.

Approaching footsteps caused her to glance up, and a wave of panic hit her when Giles came in with his registrar. Giving her a brief impersonal greeting, he turned his attention to the patient.

'Well, Richard, we managed to fix you up, I'm glad to say. How are you feeling now?'

The lad's face was stiff and swollen and he spoke with difficulty: 'Knackered. Teach me . . . to stick my nose in . . . won't it?'

'Will it? I wonder.' The surgeon gave a wry smile. He picked up the patient's charts and conferred with Peter Green on one or two points. Then he moved to check the blood transfusion, making a slight adjustment to the flow. 'We'll run this lot through fairly quickly. You'll check on his haemoglobin level tomorrow, will you, Peter?'

His dark-lashed eyes sought Joanna's, sending exquisite shivers down her spine, but there was no hint of intimacy in his look. 'Any problems?' he asked, neutrally.

'No . . . except that . . . do you think he should have some Stemetil? He's rather nauseous—it could be a strain on the wound.'

Giles wrote rapidly on the drugs sheet and handed it to her. 'There you are. And keep an eye on his blood pressure, won't you?'

When the doctors had left, Joanna breathed more easily. The confrontation had been much less awkward than she'd anticipated; all the same she was glad it was over.

She smiled at her patient. 'I'll get you those injections now, Richard, and then you can settle down to sleep again.'

Despite the half-hourly checks on his pulse and blood pressure he was sleeping when his mother arrived to see him late that afternoon, having driven from Kent. On seeing him tears sprang to her eyes. 'Poor Richard,' she said, her lips quivering. 'W-will he be permanently scarred, Nurse?'

'Oh, the scars will fade in time, Mrs Trent,' Joanna reassured her. 'He's a brave lad, isn't he?' She pulled up a chair for the woman. 'He had a sedative a while ago, so you may not get much out of him yet. Are you going back tonight, or would you like to stay? We can make arrangements.'

'Oh, that's kind of you,' his mother returned, 'but the landlady at his digs has offered to put me up.'

'Fine. Would you like some tea? I'll get you some.'

When Joanna went back with the tea Richard had woken up. There was a pallor about his nose and mouth that troubled her, although he was making light of his injuries, obviously putting on an act for his mother.

'Excuse me a minute,' she said, and stayed to check his vital signs. She was rather alarmed to find his blood pressure falling and his pulse rate rising.

After recording her findings on the chart, she advised: 'Better not stay too long this time, Mrs Trent. Richard's had a tough day. He'll be in better shape after a good night's rest.'

'All right, my dear. You know best. I'll just see what he wants me to bring in, and then I'll be going.'

Back at the nurses' station Joanna confided her fears to Eunice. 'His BP's dropped to seventy . . . '

The other girl raised her eyebrows. 'Has the transfusion tissued?'

'I don't think so . . . but I'll check it out when his mother leaves.'

Mrs Trent returned her teacup and asked what time she could visit the next day.

'Any time after two, but ring up in the morning and we'll let you know how he is,' Joanna said.

When the mother had gone Joanna went back to her patient and found him totally exhausted, his breathing laboured.

'You're looking tired, Richard. How are you feeling?'

'A bit woozy actually. It's the dope, I except.'

'Probably. Keep lying down and you'll feel better,' she soothed.

She checked the transfusion stand, and the cannula site, both of which seemed to be working

properly. She checked the dressing on his neck
wound, but there was no undue seepage from that.
She turned the handle to raise the foot of the bed
slightly, then went back to the office to bleep the
houseman.

'Steve . . . Richard Trent—the man with the
gashed jugular—his blood pressure's falling and
his pulse is one-hundred. He doesn't look too
good . . . I think he must be haemorrhaging.'

'Oh! All right—I'll be along.'

Steve arrived within a couple of minutes, looking
a little worried at the problem facing him. After
making his own checks, he scratched his head and
glanced at Joanna for inspiration. 'Peter's gone off
for the weekend. Better get GB, had I? I know he's
in ICU.'

'Yes, you better had. And get a move on,' she
added under her breath, 'I reckon it's a slipped
ligature . . . '

'Okay. But I hope you're right, or I shall look a
dope!' He sped away, leaving Joanna to explain
things to the patient.

'We think one of your internal stitches may have
slipped,' she told him smoothly. 'It may have
happened when you were sick. Don't worry,
though, the doctors can sort it out here . . . you
won't need to go back to theatre or anything.' He
was looking really distressed now and taking
sighing breaths. She reached for the oxygen mask
and held it for him. 'Have some of this . . . it'll
stop you feeling faint.'

Within a short while Steve was back with Giles,
who confirmed Joanna's suspicions.

'Yes, there seems to be a small leak in the

plumbing, old chap, but we can soon fix that, with a little local anaesthetic.' He glanced towards Joanna. 'Could we have some Lignocaine please, and a suture set?'

Having anticipated the request, she had already prepared a dressings trolley and it only remained to get the required drug from the locked cupboard. Then she made Richard ready for the procedure, and while Steve gave the injection Giles rolled back the sleeves of his blue shirt and went to scrub up.

Joanna uncovered her trolley and opened the suture pack. Giles pulled on rubber gloves and having satisfied himself that the area was properly anaesthetised, he reopened the neck wound.

'Ah! Here's the culprit,' he said, locating the bleeding point. He proceeded deftly to tie it off. 'Not hurting you, am I?' he asked the patient.

Richard said, 'No . . . the injection was the worst bit.'

With the external wound restitched, Giles stripped off his gloves and dumped them on the trolley. 'Good . . . that should give no more trouble.' He rolled down his shirt sleeves and fastened the cuffs before patting Joanna on the shoulder. 'What should we do without you?' he teased.

'What indeed?' she retorted pertly, although her cheeks burned and her heart went into overdrive when his provocative eyes met hers.

With a soft laugh he walked away talking to Steve, who was now his usual bouncy self at finding his actions justified.

Joanna pushed the infuriating surgeon to the back of her mind and concentrated on applying a fresh dressing over Richard's wound. 'Sorry we had to put you through that,' she said, 'but you should start to pick up now.' She rearranged his pillows and tidied the bedclothes. 'You're looking better already.'

He caught her hand and kissed it. 'Glad I've got you on my side,' he said, his brown eyes warm.

She gave a light laugh. 'Oh, someone else would soon have picked that up if I hadn't.' Seeing the late-night drinks coming round she glanced at her watch. 'My goodness . . . eight-thirty and no report written. I must fly.'

Wheeling her trolley to the sluice, she washed her hands and got down to her writing.

The rest of the day shift went off duty soon after the night nurses arrived, but Joanna was later in leaving as she still had a couple of things to do after giving her report.

When she walked into the lift she was confronted by Giles, also on his way home.

'Hallo,' he said. 'You still here?'

'Yes . . . that business with Richard Trent put me a bit behind.' The feelings that she had thought under control came surging back at his nearness, making her blood race.

He looked down at her with a wicked grin. 'I suppose I don't qualify for tea and sympathy tonight?'

'You certainly don't,' she retorted. They had arrived at the ground floor. 'I was the one in the hot seat tonight!'

'Yes, you did well. All right, so shall I dish out the tea and sympathy?'

'Thanks, but no thanks. I'm off to bed.'

'I'm coming your way.' He strolled along with her through the car-park until he reached his car. 'Everything all right?'

'Fine,' she said, airily.

'There seems to be a distinct chill in the air. I thought we were friends? Or should I say consenting adults?'

'Maybe my stars warned me to beware of a dark stranger,' she quipped.

'Maybe *adult* was the wrong word to use. And I'm not a stranger.'

'Whatever you like,' she returned with a honeyed smile. 'You should know by now I'm an oddball. Goodnight, Giles!' and she walked on by herself far less in control than she appeared.

The commotion inside her was robbing her limbs of strength. How could she be so idiotic as to let that superior so-and-so puncture her defences? She had no intention of letting any man influence her life in the immediate future. Neither was she going to be used as a light relief to pressure of work. No . . . from now on it was going to be strictly business between herself and Giles Beltane.

The next couple of days saw the return of Hazel Wing to Paget Ward. The porter lifted her bodily from wheelchair to bed. 'There you are m'dear, back in the land of the living,' he boomed.

'Hallo! Lovely to see you again!' Joanna pulled out the backrest and arranged the pillows and bed covers. 'You gave everyone a bit of a fright the other day.'

Hazel smiled weakly. 'So I heard . . . not that I knew much about it. I'm glad to be back here,

though. All that paraphernalia in Intensive Care
gave me the willies.'

'How does you throat feel now?'

'A wee bit sore, but not bad. I had a cup of tea
this morning. That was lovely.'

There was now only a dry dressing over her
wound as the drains and some of the clips had
already been removed. 'Well, as soon as the doctors
have been I expect we'll be removing the last of
your clips and then you'll be up and about in no
time.' Joanna put Hazel's possessions into her
locker. 'Remember Lucy? She went home on the
day of your operation . . . she sent you her good
wishes.'

Hazel was speaking quite easily now, her huski-
ness and breathlessness gone. 'She was a nice girl.
Shame about her boy-friend. I hope she'll be all
right.'

'She will in time. It's amazing how tough people
are. They bounce back eventually.' And saying
that seemed to put Joanna's own small problems
into perspective. She had her health and strength
and, compared with some of their patients, precious
little to beef about.

It was Monday . . . Admissions day. The staff
were kept on their toes making out new charts and
case histories and putting in hand the tests which
were called for. There was a constant to-ing and
fro-ing of technicians and doctors.

'Joanna, we're missing Mr Lloyd's last X-
rays . . . on your way back from lunch call in
on Mr Beltane's secretary and see if she's got them,
will you?' Sister Judd said.

Accordingly, after her meal-break, Joanna went

along to Outpatients where the secretary had an office. Tracy Kirk was a tall, well-groomed woman with an efficient manner and a very protective attitude towards her boss. It was common knowledge around the clinics that she regarded him as her own personal property. She had been devoted to Professor James, but the younger Beltane had her his adoring slave.

'Mr Thomas Lloyd's X-rays, Nurse?' she said in her plummy voice, 'no, we don't have them. They've probably gone back to X-Ray.'

'Okay, thanks.' Joanna smiled, and took herself along to the X-ray department.

The clerk searched through her files. 'No, we don't have them. They're signed out to Mr Beltane.'

Joanna sighed and went back to Miss Kirk. 'Sorry, but they say Mr Beltane still has them.'

The secretary tutted. 'I keep telling him he mustn't sit on things. Just a moment.' She knocked on the doctor's office door, disappeared inside and returned with the films and an indulgent smile. 'Here you are. If it was left to the doctors we'd never know where anything is, would we?'

Mission accomplished, Joanna had to pass through Casualty on her way back to the ward. Shaun, coming from one of the examination rooms, stopped her in her tracks.

'Hallo,' she said. 'Monday is your day here, is it?'

'Yes, usually. Come in here for a minute.' He pulled her into the doctors' office and shut the door. 'Have you thought any more about what I said?'

'What . . . about marrying you?' She grinned.

'I gave you my answer the other day, Shaun.'

She was clutching the bulky X-ray envelope to her chest. He took it from her and laid it on the desk. Then he put his arms around her and drew her close. 'Oh, come on, don't tease me, now. You know you don't mean it.'

'But I do. I'm not planning to marry any one—least of all you. And let me go, before someone comes in.'

He released her, but not before he had kissed her. 'Look, I finish here at eight. Let me at least take you out to dinner, for old times' sake?'

She hesitated. 'Oh, we-ell, all right. Anything for a quiet life.'

He beamed triumphantly. 'You can't really resist me, can you?' he said in his coaxing voice.

Joanna made a face at him. 'Oh, yes I can. I'm good at resisting these days. I'm not the push-over I used to be.'

Since Joanna was off early that day, they had arranged that she would come back to the hospital and meet him there. After a leisurely shower, she took trouble with her appearance—she washed her hair and blow-dried it into shining, casual waves, and decided on wearing a slimline turquoise blue dress and matching fun ear-rings. After all, just because she had no intention of letting this date lead to anything, that didn't mean she shouldn't look her best. And if Dr Shaun Cassidy regretted that he'd blotted his copybook with her, well, hooray!

She strolled back to Casualty and stood talking to one of the staff nurses while waiting for Shaun to finish. Then they walked to where his car was parked.

'What happened to the sports job?' she queried, eyeing his more conventional-type saloon.

'Got to foster the right image when you're a family GP,' he joked, helping her in. 'Can't have the patients thinking their doctor is a tearaway. Anyway, I've settled down now.'

'Ha-ha!' she said. 'Where are we going?'

'I've booked a table at The Chiltern. It's one of the nicest places I know—thought I'd spoil you.'

The Chiltern! That's where she'd had dinner with her father, after which she'd had that pep talk from Giles. Well, tonight was going to be nothing like as traumatic as that. She could handle Shaun very well now and he was always fun to be with.

At the hotel they sat on the paved terrace by the river and, over cocktails, chatted about old times while waiting for their table to be ready.

'Now, come on, be sensible,' he said presently. 'When shall we name the day?'

'Oh Shaun! *You* be sensible. Our little fire burned out, didn't it? And why this mad panic to get married?'

'We-ell, all the other partners in our practice are hitched up. And people prefer a family man. The trouble is, these days I don't get to meet any eligibles.'

Joanna laughed. 'I can't see that problem lasting long where you're concerned.'

The waiter came to show them to their table and when they had ordered, Shaun suddenly remarked, 'This place seems to be popular with the hospital . . . see who's over there?'

She turned to look where he nodded, and at a corner table she saw Giles with his secretary, Tracy Kirk. Quickly she averted her gaze. Giles and Tracy? Hardly his type, she would have thought. But it was no business of hers.

'Your Mrs Wing came back to us today,' she said blithely. 'Nice to know she pulled through, isn't it?'

Shaun frowned. 'Pulled through? Why, what's been going on?'

'Oh! Didn't you hear? She arrested in theatre—went to ICU for a couple of days . . . but she seems fine now.'

'Good lord! No, I hadn't heard. I haven't spoken to Beltane since . . . I must have a word with him.'

Their meal proceeded at a leisurely pace and Joanna would have enjoyed it had she not been aware that Giles knew they were there. Shaun had raised his glass in acknowledgement shortly after he'd spoken and Joanna had felt obliged to look round and smile. Giles's return smile had a distinct frost around the edges, although Shaun appeared not to notice.

While he settled the bill Joanna took the opportunity to go to the cloakroom. Coming out again, she held the door for Tracy Kirk who was about to go in.

'Hallo! Can't get away from the hospital, can we?' the secretary said merrily.

'No, it seems not,' Joanna smiled.

Giles and Shaun were talking together in the foyer. It would have seemed odd not to go over and join them. As she did so the hotel receptionist announced over the tannoy that Dr Shaun Cassidy was wanted on the telephone.

Shaun sighed, said, 'Excuse me,' and left Joanna alone with Giles.

To fill the silence which followed she said pertly, 'I see you found someone else to take care of your creature comforts.'

A satirical smile curled his lips. 'So, apparently, did you.'

'Yes. So now we're both happy.'

Bemoaning his fate, Shaun returned. 'One of my expectant mums is in difficulties. Have to hurry you, Jo.'

'You go ahead . . . we'll take Joanna home,' Giles offered.

'Will you? Thanks.' Shaun put an arm around her waist, kissed her fleetingly, said he'd be in touch, and was gone.

Her stomach churned. How *did* she keep landing in these situations? Well, at least this time she would have the redoubtable Tracy Kirk as chaperon. 'Sorry you're stuck with me,' she said, 'but you brought it on yourself.'

'Yes . . . a bad habit I seem to have got into.'

Tracy sailed back just then, and he explained.

'Oh, how lucky that we were here,' she said. 'What would you have done if we hadn't been?'

'I could've got a taxi. In fact I still can, if it's inconvenient,' Joanna suggested.

'It's not inconvenient, I need to go back to the hospital anyway,' Giles returned smoothly. 'We'll drop Tracy on the way.'

The secretary lived with her parents at Caversham, which wasn't really on the way, but that was the route he took. 'Thank you, Mr Beltane, for a delightful evening,' she gushed as he got out and courteously opened the car door for her.

He treated her to one of his mind-blowing smiles. 'My pleasure, Tracy.'

He stayed holding open the door when the secretary had gone. 'You can join me in the front now,' he said, and it was an order, not a request.

Joanna did as he asked, sitting quietly beside him, swallowing against the butterflies in her throat. Even though there was no physical contact between them, she felt the strength of his powerful body. It made her feel both secure and threatened. She clasped her hands tightly in her lap, as if holding on to herself would keep the threat at bay.

For the moment he was preoccupied with filtering into the main stream of traffic. She stole a sideways glance at him, and was bedevilled by his ability to set her senses alight, even without touching her. Oh, why hadn't she insisted on taking that taxi? Or even have gone with Shaun. Anything but putting herself in the hot seat again.

The powerful engine purred along through the summer night and presently Giles remarked, 'So, here we are again then.'

'Yes. I'm sorry if this messed up your evening with Tracy.'

'It didn't. I'd done my duty. She's a good secretary, and I like to show my appreciation occasionally.'

'Oh, I see.' She thought, *I wonder if you realise the woman adores you?* He probably did, she concluded. Men were not slow to pick up those sort of vibes.

Giles cut through her thoughts by saying: 'Coffee at my place?'

'No, thanks, I've had coffee. Anyway, I thought you were going back to the hospital?'

'It's not urgent. But you'd rather go straight home, is that it?'

'Yes, please.'

He drove on saying nothing for a while, then startled her by asking, 'How serious are things between you and Dr Cassidy?'

Joanna's cheeks flushed. 'They're not. We're just friends. Why, what has he been saying?'

He gave her an old-fashioned look. 'I'm not in his confidence, but the way he treats you I get the impression there's more to it than that.'

Pulling up outside the Nurse's Home, he switched off the engine and sat back resting his arm along the seat behind her, obviously waiting for an explanation.

CHAPTER EIGHT

IN the face of Giles's searching gaze Joanna felt compelled to admit the truth. 'Okay, so you've guessed,' she said with an uncertain laugh. 'We had an affair once . . . but that's history. We *are* just friends now.'

'Ah-ha!'

She smiled. 'Don't say that as if you think you've unearthed a skeleton in my cupboard.'

'Well, it may be over for you, Blue-eyes, but I don't think it is for him. If you mean what you say, why don't you steer clear of the fellow? Stop dangling the carrot.'

'I don't see why people can't stay friends when they decide to call it a day,' she retorted hotly.

'Debatable.' He continued to study her in that perceptive way he had and seemed in no hurry to let her go. 'How's that recalcitrant father of yours?'

'Oh, I haven't heard from him since the concert— —don't expect I shall for some time. He pops up now and again as the fancy takes him.'

'And the rest of your complicated family?'

'Fine! In fact there's going to be another wedding soon. My Aunt Beth . . . it'll be the first time for her. And the only time, I expect. She's the steady sort.'

'There aren't too many of us around.' His fingers strayed from the back of the seat to the back of her neck, tangling with the ends of her hair and sending erotic sensations down her spine.

She turned to move free of his hand and said flippantly, 'Okay, that's enough about my skeletons. What about yours?'

For a moment he didn't answer, then he said: 'Did you know I'd been married?'

There was a gruffness in his voice that had her regretting she'd asked. 'Well, yes . . . I did hear.' She hastened to explain in case he thought there'd been gossip, 'It was when you took that thorn out of my finger . . . Dorian mentioned that your wife had died of septicaemia. Giles, I'm sorry. That must have been awful for you.'

He scratched his cheek reflectively. 'Ye-es . . . it's not easy to live with the regrets you have afterwards. We take people too much for granted . . . and then it's too late. Anyway,' he went on, snapping out of his mood, 'work is a splendid restorative. That, and the occasional counter-irritant,' he added jokingly.

His fingers found the back of her neck again, sending further quivers of delight through her veins. He nodded towards the Nurses' Home. 'I thought you were moving out of this place?'

'We are—next Saturday.' Silence hung in the air between them. Then she said. 'Well, I suppose it's time I went in.

'Yes, I suppose you better had. And since I'm not treading on anyone's toes . . . '

His arm dropped to her shoulders and he leaned towards her, pulling her closer. *No! Please,* she thought desperately, her heart in her mouth, but it was too late for resistance. His lips were on hers. She couldn't *not* have responded, even if she'd wanted to. Of their own free will her arms went round his neck. Her very bones seemed to liquefy as his mouth teased hers, tantalizing and seductive. It lasted for some time, and when he finally drew away she felt deprived.

'Thank you. That was the best part of the evening,' he said with a roguish grin.

Joanna matched his frivolous tone. 'Better not let your secretary hear you say that. Goodnight!' and she slipped out of the car and ran up to her room.

Her blood was at fever-pitch, her limbs trembling. How could she ever have thought she was in love with Shaun? That had been child's play compared with the earth-moving sensations Giles stirred in her. And to him it was just a pleasurable exercise! *Damn you, Giles,* she muttered, furious with herself and with him. *Stay out of my life!*

On Wednesday morning Joanna drove her car to the station. The car-park was full but she managed to find a space in a quiet street nearby. The train journey to Paddington took only twenty-five minutes, as against two hours if she'd gone by road, and then there would have been the greater problem of parking in London.

Arriving at noon, she took the Underground to Marble Arch and made for the reception lounge of the Cumberland Hotel. Beth was there waiting for her, looking smart in a floral silk dress under a boxy white jacket. They hugged each other affectionately.

'Beth, you're absolutely glowing,' Joanna said,

smiling at the other's radiant face. 'So this is what love does for you!'

Beth laughed. 'Exciting, isn't it? I never thought it would happen to me.'

They made their way to the Carvery where, over a leisurely meal with a bottle of wine, they exchanged news.

'Tell me more about this wonderful John, then,' Joanna said. 'When are you going to tie the knot?'

'Well, we're going to wait until your mother and Malcolm come home, and then we'll sort things out between us.'

'And where will you live?'

'In the flat over his shop to begin with . . . John hasn't any children, so there's no difficulties there. Now what about you, Jo?' Beth asked. 'No new man on the horizon yet?'

Joanna could always talk to Beth. Although they weren't the same generation, they seemed to speak the same language. She wrinkled her nose. 'We-ell, Shaun has surfaced in my neck of the woods again. He's a GP now, and does his stint in Casualty at the hospital. And, you'll never guess! He's asked me to marry him.'

'Good heavens!' Beth's eyes widened. 'Are you going to?'

'No, I'm not. He's had it.' Joanna paused. 'In any case, I've decided to concentrate on my career for now.'

'Well, that's not a bad idea. There's plenty of time for you. You'll come out of this patch,' Beth said understandingly.

'What patch?'

Beth smiled. 'Come on, I know you. Bet you've

been chewing your fingernails, what with your dad and his new dolly-bird, and Shaun. And now there's me walking out on you.'

'Don't be so ridiculous! I can't be more pleased for you . . . I only hope your John knows what a treasure he's getting,' Joanna returned cheerfully. She downed the last of her rosé. 'Right, let's have a mooch around the shops now, and then we'll have some tea before we go to the theatre.'

Much later, having laughed their way through a domestic comedy at the Haymarket, they emerged lighthearted from the theatre into the glittering London nightlife. Pavements milled with cosmopolitan crowds while taxis, cars and buses dodged the jay-walkers spilling on to the road.

Beth linked her arm through Joanna's. 'Don't go back tonight, you'll be so late. Come home to Chelsea and get an early train in the morning,' she invited.

'Okay . . . I might as well,' Joanna agreed. 'I'm not on till one tomorrow. I had to leave my car in a side street, but it should be all right.'

It made a pleasant end to the evening to go back to the old place together, and over a late-night drink they talked about family matters and Beth's future.

In bed in her old room Joanna thought about her own past with mixed pleasure and regrets. As Giles had pointed out, she could have been a lot worse off. At least she hadn't been a tug-of-love victim like some of the children one read about. And she'd been able to follow her own career without interference from anyone. Her future was in her own hands, so she had best stop wallowing in nostalgia and get on with living.

She caught the eleven a.m. train back from Paddington the following day. Her trusty Fiesta was still where she had left it and she made towards it cheerfully. On reaching it, however, she discovered to her dismay that someone had backed into her—there was a sizeable dent in the front bumper, plus a cracked headlamp.

'Oh, hell!' she exploded, viewing the damage. She patted the bonnet affectionately. 'Poor baby!' But maddening though the damage was, the car should still be drivable. With a resigned sigh Joanna unlocked the door and slid behind the wheel. She put her key in the ignition and turned, but there was absolutely no response whatever—the engine appeared completely dead. This was ridiculous! The tank was half full, the battery barely a month old . . .

Groaning with despair she glanced at her watch. There was certainly no time to do anything about it now if she wasn't to be late for work. She'd have to get someone out to look at it tonight.

With a sigh of exasperation she relocked the car and went in search of a bus or taxi. But there was a dearth of taxis and no sign of a bus. The minutes ticked by as she waited in the lengthening queue with growing impatience.

At long last a bus appeared in the distance, but ahead of it and approaching fast was a familiar BMW. Recognising Giles at the wheel, Joanna waved frantically. He cruised to a stop a couple of yards ahead of her and she ran to catch up with him. 'Are you going to the hospital?'

'Yes, hop in. What's the panic?' he asked, driving smoothly on.

'Some stupid oaf has bashed into my car!' she fumed. 'I couldn't get it to start . . . and I'm due on at lunchtime.'

He gave her a quick sideways glance. 'Are you all right?'

'Oh, yes. I wasn't in it at the time.' She explained what had happened.

'I suppose you were badly parked.'

'I wasn't!' she returned indignantly, 'I was tucked away in a cul-de-sac. The trouble is,' she went on, 'I really need it this weekend. On Saturday we're moving out to Pangbourne.'

'Perhaps it's something simple, like an electrical fault.' He paused. 'Would you like me to look at it?'

She glanced at him in surprise. 'Can you spare the time? I know you're busy . . . ?'

'Yes, very busy. But you're a constant thorn in my flesh, young woman. Shall we say some time this evening?'

'All right, and thanks . . . although I shan't be free until nine-thirty.'

They were skirting the hospital now and he drew up outside the Nurses' Home. 'I'll pick you up here at ten.'

'Great!' She smiled warmly as she got out of the car. 'And thanks for the lift . . . you saved my life.'

'You forgot to say . . . *again!*' he reminded her wryly.

By one o'clock Joanna was back on duty and personal matters had to be forgotten while she concentrated on catching up with ward affairs. As always when returning from days off, there were new patients to get to know and the progress of others to be followed through.

Hazel Wing, the thyroidectomy patient, was so much improved that she was for discharge the following day.

Richard Trent was also back on his feet and would be going home later that day. He had made rapid strides since having the slipped ligature in his neck replaced. His bruises were fading and his stab wounds healing well. In the treatment room Joanna removed the last of his stitches.

'There you are, Richard, you can hardly see the join!'

He swung his legs over the side of the couch and grinned at her. 'Is that one of your stock remarks? Like, "You're back in the ward and you're fine," ' he mimicked.

Joanna laughed softly. 'You're here to prove it, aren't you?'

'Thanks to you. And I really mean that.'

'Oh, go on! Are you going home to convalesce, or will you stay at your digs?'

'That depends.' Richard hesitated. 'Have you got a boy-friend?' he queried.

She could guess what he was leading up to. 'Yes, I have,' she fibbed.

'Pity. Would I have been in with a chance?'

'Not a hope!' She flashed him a friendly smile and carried on tidying up her used materials. 'We get so many handsome heroes passing though our hands, we get spoiled for choice.'

He sighed and looked soulful. 'When you think

your number's up, and then you wake to find a
blue-eyed blonde holding your hand, that's a very
emotive experience.'

Joanna chuckled. 'Well, go and write a poem
about it and let me get on with my work.'

Her next job was to show Sally, the new student,
how to prepare a tincture of Benzoin inhalation
for Mr Lloyd. It was the patient's third post-
operative day after removal of his gall bladder,
and having been a heavy smoker he was rather
chesty.

'He was awfully grumpy when we bathed him
this morning,' Sally said, sounding apprehensive.

'Well, a cholecystectomy is a painful operation,'
Joanna remarked. 'He's had his nasogastric tube
out now, so perhaps that will improve his temper.'

They took the steaming bowl along on a tray.
'Here's your inhalation, Mr Lloyd,' Joanna said
pleasantly. 'Let's sit you up a bit first, shall we?'

He was a big man with a pale, fleshy face and
an aggrieved expression. 'Careful,' he growled as
the nurses, one on either side, helped him forward
and plumped up his pillows.

'Sorry,' Joanna said gently, 'I know it's painful
to move, but it has to be done.' They positioned
the bed-table in front of him and put the inhalation
in place. 'Do you find this helps your breathing?'

'A drop of the hard stuff would be a damn sight
better,' Mr Lloyd grumbled.

Joanna smiled. 'I'm afraid that's not on the
menu today.' She placed the towel over his face.
'We'll be back to tidy you up before visitors.'

Next they helped other patients back to bed,
attended to various toilet needs and charted fluids.

Joanna noticed an infusion bag which needed changing.

'Sally,' she said, 'go and take that inhalation from Mr Lloyd before we forget,' and she went off towards the clinical room.

A moment later there was a loud clatter and sounds of a disturbance from down the ward. Looking out to see what had happened, Joanna saw Sister Judd speeding in the direction of Mr Lloyd's bed. Sally, wet and tearful, was stooping to retrieve the inhalation bowl from the floor.

'What was all that about?' she asked Richard, who had been an interested onlooker.

'He just chucked that bowl of stuff at the poor kid, the old devil!'

'Oh dear!' She hurried to see if she could help and found Sister Judd giving the patient a piece of her mind.

'Now, Mr Lloyd, that was very naughty of you. How do you expect us to keep our nurses if you behave like that? You're a grown man, not a schoolboy—you should know better.' Sister turned to the distraught student. 'All right Sally, off you go and get yourself into a dry uniform . . . and ask Agnes to come and swab the floor, will you, or we shall all be slipping over.'

'I'll bring a clean counterpane, Sister,' Joanna went back down the ward with the unhappy junior. 'Don't worry, Sally,' she consoled. 'I had a urinal chucked at me once! You'll survive.'

'I f-felt such a fool, with everyone looking on,' the girl faltered. 'He yelled at me, and I'd only stopped to pour someone else a drink . . . '

'Well, you'll have the other patients' sympathy.

And we don't get many like him, thank goodness.'
Joanna frowned. 'Funny, him turning like that. He
seemed okay when he first came in.'

Taking a fresh quilt from the linen cupboard she
returned to help Sister Judd clean up Mr Lloyd's
soiled bed. He was still looking dour, complaining
that he shouldn't have been kept waiting.

'We do have other patients, you know,' the Sister
reminded him primly, 'but we'll say no more about
it.'

Agnes trundled along with her mop and bucket
and a few good-natured grumbles. Joanna gathered
up the wet quilt and walked back down the ward
with her senior.

'Some people!' sighed the Sister, tutting in disap-
proval. 'All right, Joanna, you can let the visitors
in now and then go to tea.'

In the coffee bar Joanna was pleased to find Gail
whom she hadn't seen for a few days. It being
fresh in her mind she mentioned the spot of bother
on the ward with Mr Lloyd.

'There's something a bit odd about him . . .
he's got these pale blue staring eyes. They give me
the shivers. Oh well,' she shrugged it off and went
on to talk about her day in town. 'I stayed overnight, and when I got back this morning I found
that some idiot had clobbered my car. I couldn't
get a peep out of it . . . I can't think why—the
damage didn't seem all that serious.'

Gail raised her neat eyebrows. 'Did you leave
your lights on and run the battery down?'

'No, it wasn't dark when I left. Anyway, there I

was waiting for a bus or taxi when GB came along and gave me a lift.'

'That was useful. So what are you going to do about the car?' Gail hesitated. 'Dorian did ask me out for a drink tonight, but maybe he'd . . . '

'No sweat. Giles has offered to run me back there to see if he can fix it,' Joanna told her. 'He's picking me up at ten.'

'Oh, nice of him. But then, he's like that, isn't he?'

'Couldn't have happened at a worse time, though,' Joanna brooded, 'just when we're about to move house.'

'Not to worry,' Gail said. 'We've still got my car, and maybe it won't take too long to put yours right.'

'It seemed as dead as a dodo,' Joanna said gloomily.

At nine-thirty she returned to her room to wash and change. The night was chilly and overcast, so she dressed in jeans and a blue sweat shirt and went downstairs to await Giles's arrival.

He, too, had changed his formal attire for hip-hugging jeans and a casual cotton-knit sweater, and sitting beside him in the car, her body reacted with its usual clamour to his potent magnetism.

'This is really good of you,' she said, swallowing.

The dark-lashed grey-green eyes met hers equivocally. 'Yes, isn't it? I'm a glutton for punishment.'

She grinned. 'I don't know what you can do . . . except perhaps recommend me a good mechanic, if you know of one.'

'Let's wait and see, shall we? Tell me where to go.'

She directed him through the town to the quiet cul-de-sac where she was parked. He pulled up alongside the yellow Fiesta and they both alighted.

'Right. Let's have the bonnet up, and don't switch on until I tell you,' Giles ordered.

Joanna slipped behind the wheel and released the bonnet catch. He raised the lid, propped it open and leaned over to investigate. 'What happened to your battery?' he called.

Joanna frowned. 'Nothing, as far as I know.'

'Well, you haven't got one. It isn't here.'

'*What?*' She leapt from her seat and ran to look. An empty space and dangling leads met her eyes. 'Good grief!' she exclaimed. 'Someone must've lifted it—the rotten so-and-so!'

Giles shut down the lid. 'We'd best go and buy you another.'

'I wonder how they got the bonnet open?' she puzzled as they went in search of a late-night service station.

'Oh, that wouldn't present any problem to a determined villain. Nothing missing from inside?'

'I didn't check, but there wasn't much of value . . . except a few cassettes. I suppose I was lucky they didn't pinch the car as well.'

She insisted on paying for the new battery herself, glad that she had her credit card in her shoulder bag. Within ten minutes Giles had installed it and the terminals were fixed into place. Now when she turned the ignition, the car immediately came to life.

'Oh, brilliant!' she exclaimed in delight, and jumping out, she brought him a duster to wipe his hands on. 'Giles . . . I'm very grateful.'

He closed the bonnet lid, cleaned his fingers and eyed her with amusement. 'Then show me.'

Joanna hesitated, hypnotized by his powerful charisma, trying to stifle the urgent feelings even the sound of his voice could arouse in her.

'*Well?*' he murmured seductively.

She reached up to kiss him. And for a glorious heart-stopping moment his arms wrapped around her while their mouths united. She could imagine nothing more exquisite than giving herself to him completely. Then discretion prevailed and she pulled free. 'Debt discharged!' she declared.

'Actually, that's not quite what I had in mind,' he returned, teasing. 'I was thinking of omelettes. How about it?'

Her colour rose, but she laughed. 'Oh, no! Not tonight—it's too late for that.'

He didn't try to persuade her. 'Off you go then—and *please* try to stay out of trouble. You put untold strains on my patience.' He shut her into the car and waved her off.

Joanna drove herself back to the Nurses' Home, her thoughts in chaos. Against her will she was hopelessly drawn to Giles, and it was fairly obvious that she did something for him, if only physically. But there would need to be very powerful forces at work to break through the barrier of his career, so it was no good harbouring romantic dreams.

It could even be that he was still faithful to the memory of his wife. Whichever way Joanna looked at it offered no solution. It was pointless to read anything into his little kindnesses. As Gail had said, he was like that. And the fact that it made her love him was just too bad.

In any case, she wasn't prepared to embark on another fruitless love affair, was she? That would be courting disaster. She should have learned that lesson from her parents.

CHAPTER NINE

'How did you get on last night, Jo?' Gail enquired. They were walking over to the hospital together early on Friday morning. 'Was Giles able to do anything about your car?'

'Yes, luckily. Would you believe it? . . . some rotten blighter had pinched my battery! We had to go and buy a new one. Everything was okay once he'd fitted it, apart from the front headlight which I shall have to get fixed. So that wasn't too bad, I suppose.'

'Men do have their uses,' Gail allowed. 'Good . . . so we can pack up our stuff in the morning and get ourselves over to Swallows. I talked to Pam last night. They're off today. She's going to leave the keys under the flower-pot behind the side-gate. You've got the weekend off, haven't you?'

'Yes . . . Beryl wanted time off for the Henley Regatta, so we swapped. Oh, I'm really looking forward to moving; hope your cousin doesn't come back for ages.'

'Well . . . she thought about a year,' Gail said, 'but anything can happen between now and then.' Pushing through the swing-doors into the hospital they joined the many other members of staff arriving for early duty. ' 'Bye! See you at lunchtime,' and Gail turned in the direction of the theatre wing.

Joanna took the lift to Paget Ward, deposited her cloak and bag in the staff room and joined the day nurses gathered in the office to hear Delphine's report.

It appeared to have been an average sort of night with no spectacular happenings. There had been only one problem. 'Meester Lloyd . . . 'e was very restless and noisy . . . 'e pulled out his IV at two a.m. But it was the last pack and nearly run through, so the duty houseman said it wasn't worth putting back.'

'Yes, he'll be on free fluids from today,' nodded Sister Judd. She narrowed her eyes. 'He wasn't throwing things again, was he?'

'No, but he has found the short temper. Poof!' and Delphine rolled her big dark eyes.

Most of them smiled, but Student Nurse Sally Armstrong looked anxious. 'I'll be glad when he's gone,' she said with feeling.

'So shall we all at this rate,' the Sister agreed, 'but we have to make allowances. Illness affects people in many different ways; they often behave completely out of character. Never mind, Sally, you can stay clear of him today. We'll let Joanna handle him.'

'Thanks a bunch!' Joanna said drily.

The busy morning ritual got under way, and when the dust of bedmaking and ward cleaning had settled, Joanna started on her dressings.

'See to Mr Lloyd first,' Sister Judd advised. 'Call me when you're ready and I'll come and look at his wound.'

Having prepared her trolley, Joanna wheeled it to the bedside and drew the screening curtains. She greeted him with a cheerful, 'Good morning! And how are you today?'

'Damn glad to get rid of that drip!' he grunted.

'Yes, I'm sure. You'll be able to move about more now, won't you? I have to change your dressing, but Sister is going to have a look at it first.'

She noticed that he was very fidgety and breathing heavily, and he kept brushing at his face as though there was something on it. Not that she could see anything, but he was perspiring a lot, so perhaps it was that worrying him. 'We'll be sitting you out presently. That's progress, isn't it?' she chatted.

He brushed at his face again and gazed past her with a vacant look in his eyes, seeming not to hear what she said.

Joanna went to wash her hands and call Sister. 'He's sweating like mad although his temperature's normal. But I suppose it is a bit warm in here.'

The Sister pursed her lips and made no comment. She consulted the temperature chart at the foot of the bed before coming to inspect the wound site. It was clean and dry with just a slight oozing from the drain.

'Well, that looks very nice, Mr Lloyd,' she said. 'I think you can spray that, Joanna, and just put a dry dressing over the drain site.' She stayed until the job was done and afterwards helped Joanna tidy the bed and rearrange his pillows.

He had submitted to the proceedings with a certain amount of irritation, but by and large it had gone better than Joanna expected, perhaps because the Sister was there. 'Are you hot?' she asked. 'We could leave off a blanket.'

He waved his hand dismissively. 'Do what you like. But I could use a drink.'

Up until now there had been no jug on his locker as his fluids by mouth had been restricted.

'What would you like . . . a cup of tea?' suggested Sister.

'Tea?' He shook his head, then gave a queer semblance of a smile. 'My wife's going to bring me in some . . . lemonade today.'

'Oh! Well, we can find you some squash if that's what you'd prefer.'

Tidying back the bed curtains, they left him still brushing at imaginary things on his clothing and his face.

Sister Judd looked thoughtful. 'He's behaving a bit strangely, isn't he? Humour him as much as possible. Take him a drink, but don't bother with the inhalations since he's sweating. We'll see what the doctors have to say when they come.'

After she had cleared away her trolley and washed her hands yet again Joanna took along the promised lemon drink. She poured a glass for him. 'Here you are, Mr Lloyd, you can drink as much as you like now.'

He bared his smoker's teeth in a peculiar kind of grin. In fact it was so eerie it sent a shiver over her scalp.

In the canteen at lunchtime she discussed the patient with Gail. 'Remember that man I told you about yesterday? Well, he's really strange. He seemed quite normal before he had his op, but now it's almost as if he's had a personality change. It's creepy.'

'Perhaps he's a manic depressive,' joked Gail.

'Gee, thanks! Any more bright ideas?' They both laughed and Joanna went on: 'There's no suggestion of anything like that in his history. Oh well, perhaps I'm making something out of nothing. I don't suppose he's the last funny customer we'll have to deal with.'

Returning to the ward she found plenty going on. Patients were being helped back to bed after lunch, and pressure care and TPRs being attended to. Giles, Peter and Steve were in the office consulting with Sister Judd and about to start their round. Beryl had already been assigned to wheel out the notes trolley, so Joanna went off to dispense the two p.m. drugs.

It was a job she quite enjoyed since it gave an opportunity to talk to all the patients. With Sally as her assistant, they consulted medication sheets, measured doses, counted out pills and waited while they were swallowed, crushed up tablets for those who found swallowing difficult.

Although concentrating on the job in hand, Joanna could not help being conscious of Giles's presence on the ward. She caught snatches of his deeply resonant voice, noticed his courtesy to the patients, and the virile grace of his lithe limbs as he went from bed to bed.

He was all she could ever have wished for in a man—strong, dependable and exciting, sending erotic feelings coursing through her. Totally committed to his work, alas. And it was a sensible decision she had made last night in accepting that fact, she reminded herself. Involuntarily she sighed and made a determined effort to shut him out of her mind.

They were nearing the bay that Mr Lloyd occupied with three other patients when one of the men called urgently: 'Nurse! Tom's going queer . . . you'd better come quick!'

Hastily Joanna shut down the drugs trolley and ran to see what was wrong. She found Mr Lloyd shaking and agitated, his eyes wild, his face grotesquely contorted.

'What is it, Mr Lloyd?' she asked anxiously.

The pale blue eyes that turned on her were terror-filled. It was as though he were seeing the Devil himself. He let out an anguished cry and his massive hands flew for her throat.

She heard Sally scream. She heard the opposite patient yell: 'Help! Stop him, someone!' But the big hands were squeezing, squeezing and shaking her like a rag doll. And she couldn't prise the hands away. Everything began to spin . . . her legs were collapsing . . . her head was going to burst . . . it finally exploded into darkness.

As the light slowly returned, Joanna's head reeled. She swallowed painfully and put her hands to her bruised throat. Memory surfaced, and she shuddered, reliving the nightmarish moment. Now she was sitting on one of the ward chairs, although how she had got there she didn't know.

Beryl's arm was round her shoulders and she was murmuring soothingly, 'You're all right,

Jo . . . you just blacked out for half a sec.'

There was a buzz of concern and sympathy around the ward. Curtains screened Mr Lloyd's bed and the low rumble of male voices could be heard as Giles and his colleagues dealt with the deranged patient.

Then Giles emerged from behind the curtains and came towards her. He was totally in control, tough as steel, and the sight of him gladdened her heart. She wanted to cry.

He stooped to her level and took her hand in his. 'That was a nasty moment, Joanna. Are you okay?'

She nodded, fighting to control her quivering lips. 'Wh-what was wrong with him?'

'Acute alcohol withdrawal. He was hallucinating. We've given him some Heminevrin.'

'DTs?' Joanna said, the truth dawning.

'Yes. His supply has been curtailed since he's been in here. Now we know his problem we can handle it.'

Sister Judd tidied back the curtains to reveal Mr Lloyd now quietly sedated. 'Dear me!' she sighed, shaking her head, 'I do wish people would tell us about these things.'

'Half the alcoholics don't realise they have a problem,' put in Peter Green.

The Sister nodded. 'You have a point there, Doctor.' Her brow puckered as she looked at her staff nurse. 'Well, Joanna, how do you feel, my dear?'

'Oh, just a bit wobbly. I'll be all right in a minute.' She tried to stand up, but promptly sat down again.

'Had I better get a wheelchair, Sister?' Beryl suggested.

'No need for that—she's only a lightweight.' Giles scooped her up in his strong arms and carried her the length of the ward where he sat her down in the treatment room. 'Nearly lost one of your nine lives, didn't you?' He ran his fingers gently over her neck and tutted.

She raised a wan smile. 'You say the nicest things!'

The Sister had bustled in after them. 'Beryl's making you a cup of tea, dear. And what do you think, Mr Beltane, some linctus to ease her throat?'

He nodded. 'Then she ought to go off for the rest of the day. Can you manage?'

'Oh yes, we've a double shift on until four-thirty.'

'Fine, and I should send someone over with her, just to make sure she's okay.'

Beryl came in with the tea and everyone else returned to their work. 'Sister says when you feel up to it I'm to take you back to your room. I'll fetch your cloak and bag.'

'I'll be all right on my own,' Joanna said. 'You don't have to come.'

'GB has ordered, mate, and don't you forget it,' grinned Beryl. 'What did it feel like, being swept off your feet by Mr Universe?'

Joanna sipped her tea and swallowed carefully. 'Pity I wasn't in the right state of mind to appreciate it.' But that wasn't quite true. It had been sheer heaven to be held safe and close against his powerful body. Even despite her ordeal she had been aware of the thrilling, warm male scent of him and the touch of his hands on her skin.

Later, back in her room she stripped off her uniform and flopped on the bed in her dressing-gown. It was amazing how exhausted she felt. That, she supposed as she dozed off, must be the delayed effect of the shock.

At six o'clock she was awakened by a knock on her door and Gail looked in. 'Hallo,' she said with a sympathetic smile, coming to sit on the bed. 'Giles asked me to keep an eye on you. You okay?'

Joanna heaved herself up and sighed. 'Oh yes, I'm fine now. I just felt completely whacked. You heard what happened?'

'Yes, you were saying there was something queer about that patient, weren't you? What a carry on!'

'Mmmm . . . trust me to be the one on the receiving end! Lucky there were plenty of people around.'

Gail raised her eyes to the ceiling. 'Training in self-defence should be part of a nurse's curric-ulum. Well, do you feel like something to eat? I don't suppose you want to go out.'

'No, not really . . . I'm not awfully hungry. A bowl of soup would suit me. My throat aches a bit.'

'Okay. I've got some packets. I'll do it, you stay put. We'll have a nice relaxed evening and perhaps start our packing, eh? Moving day tomorrow . . . hooray!'

She disappeared and presently came back with

two bowls of tomato soup topped with grated cheese, and the remains of a sliced wholemeal loaf. 'There you are, that should slip down all right.'

'Thanks, you're a pal,' Joanna said gratefully.

Having eaten and discussed the events of the day, neither of them felt much like starting to pack.

Joanna said, 'I can't be bothered to do anything else tonight. Think I'll have a bath and go to bed.'

Gail stretched and ran her hands through her long brown hair. 'Okay, I'll leave you to it. Anyway, there'll be no great rush tomorrow, so long as we're out by twelve-thirty. See you in the morning, then.'

Returning from the bathroom, Joanna smoothed some cream over the pressure marks around her neck. Studying herself in the mirror she marvelled that she looked the same as ever. But she wasn't the same. She had been face-to-face with death. Maybe she was over-dramatizing, but supposing she had been attacked alone on night duty, for instance? She might well be dead. It struck her forcibly how precarious life was . . . how easily it could be snuffed out . . . how little time there might be to let people know that you cared.

In a reflective mood she slipped into bed and switched off her bedside lamp, her mind full of profound thoughts about life and death. Those anonymous people you passed in the street every day, you never really knew what went on behind their seemingly ordinary faces; the hidden pressures that made them what they were. And the relatives who visited dying patients in hospital, how many of them, like Giles, were left with thoughts of the things they had meant to say and didn't?

It came home to her what Giles must have suffered when his wife had been snatched away without warning. Well, from now on she was never going to take people for granted. She wouldn't hide her loving feelings, and she would be less critical. She felt glad that Giles had prompted her to support her father that time; it was good to know that they had parted on a pleasant note.

Her last conscious thought was of the senior surgeon who made her feel both safe and threatened. Safe, because he always seemed to be there when she needed someone. Threatened, because he had only to look at her to start a fire in her loins.

The following morning both girls were up early. After having coffee together they decided to bring their cars round to the front of the building in order to load up.

Back in her room Joanna lifted down her travel bags from the top of the wardrobe and began the task of emptying drawers, taking posters off walls, packing books into a carton.

'Isn't it amazing the junk you collect!' said Gail, pausing with a load of things in her arms. 'We could do with a pair of those manly biceps you were talking about.'

She went on down the corridor and Joanna

heard her talking to someone. Most likely one of the other nurses, she concluded, and carried on clearing out her bedside cabinet.

Presently a firm rat-tat on her wide open door made her glance up, and her heart lurched when she saw Giles framed in the doorway. He looked endearingly rugged in casual trousers and a fawn crew neck sweater over a gingham shirt. 'Hallo!' she said. 'What are you doing here?'

'I came to see how you were. No bad dreams during the night, I hope?'

His deep voice sent delicious tremors down her spine and she strove to suppress the crazy desires that shot through her. 'No . . . no bad dreams.' She flashed him a self-conscious smile. 'Quite the reverse in fact. I felt so lucky to be alive, I made umpteen good resolutions.'

'You did, did you?' His curvy mouth twitched. 'And what were they?'

She grinned. 'Oh, definitely not for publication.'

'May I come in?'

'Please do. Excuse the mess—it looks like the last day of the sales in here. Do you want to sit down?' She swept a pile of clothes off the only chair, but he chose to perch on the side of her bed. His eyes were watching her every movement, and she didn't quite know what next to say or do. She said: 'Well, how is Mr Lloyd?'

'Oh, he'll be all right now we've got him controlled. I must confess,' he went on with a wry smile, 'there have been times when I've felt like wringing your little neck myself, but I do take exception to someone else trying to do it.'

She widened her eyes in mock indignation. 'Then I shall certainly not cook *you* any more omelettes.'

'Is that a threat or a promise?' He caught at her hand as she attempted to get on with her clearing up. 'Slow down a minute, for goodness' sake.' He pulled her down beside him. 'You've got all day, haven't you?'

'Not really . . . we have to be out by twelve-thirty; there are other people coming in. Anyway, we have to get to the house to feed the cat.'

'What cat is that?' he asked.

She explained about the pet that went with the house. 'It's a dear little thing—Siamese. We never had pets at home . . . ' She paused, suddenly conscious of his steady scrutiny, and when their eyes met, the expression in his set her blood racing. Her cheeks flamed.

'Well, go on,' he murmured, smiling.

To her relief the moment was interrupted as Gail came back, looked in and grinned. 'Giles, are you holding up the good work?'

Joanna jumped up. 'Yes, I can't sit here gassing to you. Make yourself useful and carry something down for me.'

'That's all I seem to have been doing ever since I met you, making myself useful,' he quipped.

'Mr Wonderful!' she returned with a cheeky grin. 'I do appreciate it.'

'Was that one of your good resolutions, to seduce me with flattery?'

She wrinkled her nose at him, bent down and zipped up a large, well-filled travel bag. 'Take this, will you?'

He rose and ruffled her blonde locks. 'I don't usually take orders from women, but I'll make an exception this once.' Then he picked up the bag and she followed him down to the street with her electric kettle and a box of oddments.

He stayed to make a few more sorties for both girls until all their possessions were safely installed in their cars. 'Sorry I can't come and help you unload the other end,' he said, consulting his wristwatch, 'but I've got a luncheon appointment.'

'We'll manage,' returned Gail cheerfully. 'Thanks for your help.'

'Yes, thanks,' added Joanna. 'We were just wishing for an extra pair of hands, and there you were. Must have been telepathy.'

He curbed a smile. 'I call it taking advantage of my saintly nature!' He strolled off in the direction of the hospital car-park.

The girls went back to have a last look around their rooms before handing in their keys to the warden. Then they set off in convoy towards Pangbourne.

Keeping Gail's blue Volkswagen in view, Joanna took careful note of the route from the hospital so that she would know the way when she was on her own. Leaving the town for leafy Berkshire roads, they drew up some twenty minutes later in the drive of their new home. There was a welcoming pint of milk on the doorstep and a printed leaflet from the milkman advertising everything from potatoes to yoghurt.

After unloading their possessions, the girls opened windows and made themselves at home.

Gail's cousin had left a few useful items in the fridge and quite a few groceries in the cupboards.

'She said she'd leave us enough to be getting on with,' Gail said, investigating. 'There's bacon . . . I'm quite peckish. Are you?'

Having started the day with only a mug of coffee, Joanna was quite hungry too, so they settled for a hot bacon sandwich before starting to unpack.

They were finishing their snack at the breakfast bar when the cat-flap clicked and in ran the Siamese cat. It miaowed plaintively, rubbing itself around Joanna's legs. She picked it up and fondled its silky ears. 'Hallo, puss. Aren't you sweet?'

'Wants *her* lunch, I expect. Half a tin of cat food, and some water, Pam said.'

'I thought cats drank milk?'

'Apparently not this one.' Gail found a tin of food in a cupboard and spooned some into the dish provided. Then she filled the drinking bowl with fresh water.

They watched the little creature nibble daintily around the edge, but she ate only a small part of the meal and then proceeded to wash herself vigorously.

Joanna was intrigued. 'She doesn't seem very hungry, does she?'

'She catches birds and things, so I've been warned,' Gail said regretfully, 'but that's a natural instinct, I suppose.'

Opening the back door, Joanna wandered around the small but well-tended garden, sniffing at stocks and old-fashioned cloves. She cut some sprays of a sweetly-scented pink rambler rose, found a vase for them and put them on the sideboard. After the institutional atmosphere of the Nurses' Home it was going to be bliss living here in freedom.

The day passed quickly as they settled into their new surroundings, finding out where things were and finding places for their personal belongings.

That evening they decided to sample the fare at one of the local pubs and settled on a pleasant black-beamed inn. They ate at a table on the terrace—quiche with crisp salad and a bottle of wine—and afterwards took a stroll along the riverbank.

Lawned gardens on the opposite bank stretched down to the water's edge where pleasure-craft were anchored at private moorings. Further on the river surged in savage splendour over the weir and wooded slopes rose against the skyline in the pale dusk. It was all quite idyllic.

Joanna sighed dreamily. ' "A book of verse beneath the bough, a jug of wine, a loaf of bread—and thou!" ' she quoted.

'Oh, yes? What brought all that on?' Gail laughed. 'Anyone would think you were in love.'

'I am . . . with life, at the moment. Don't forget, I wouldn't be here if Mr Lloyd had had his way yesterday!'

It was a plausible explanation, if not the correct one. Actually Joanna had been thinking of Giles—in fact he had never been far from her thoughts all day. It made her feel really good that he'd bothered to come and see how she was.

Naturally, he would have been concerned about such a thing happening to any of the staff on the ward. All the same, he needn't have come himself. He had already asked Gail to keep an eye on her. Joanna sighed as unanswered questions filled her head. Just to be in the same room with him set her senses alight, but it was ridiculous to imagine he felt the same.

'Well, you *are* here,' Gail cut in on her thoughts, 'and a miss is as good as a mile,' she said cheerfully, 'so don't go all soulful on me.' She slapped at a gnat on her leg. 'Come on, let's get back before we get bitten to death.'

Later, back at the house they got down to deciding on what to put into the kitty for household running expenses. Then there were numerous telephone calls to be made to let friends know of their change of address and telephone number. Finally they relaxed in front of the television to watch the late-night film before going to bed.

Joanna's room had a pastel-pink duvet on the double bed, with sprigged Laura-Ashley style curtains at the windows. There was a long, white-painted wardrobe with a recessed dressing-table. The overall effect was light and pleasing. She lay for a while letting impressions sink in, toying with colour schemes she might go for if ever she got to furnishing a house herself.

That was something she would have had the chance to do had she agreed to marry Shaun. But there was more to being married than setting up home. The first essential was to find the right partner; and right partners were hard to come by. As her own family had proved, all the possessions in the world counted for nothing otherwise.

Her thoughts came back to Giles. Sooner or later their paths would diverge, as so often happened in hospital life. Perhaps when she had become a staid nursing officer and he had rooms in Harley Street they might come across each other some time, and he would remember the girl whose neck he had wanted to wring.

Joanna smiled ruefully, switched out her light and fell asleep still thinking of him.

CHAPTER TEN

On Monday morning Gail left the house earlier than Joanna, as she had a dental appointment before starting work.

Soon after she had gone the telephone rang and, on answering it, Joanna was surprised to hear her mother's voice at the other end of the line.

'Is that you, Jo? I'm home, darling.'

'Mum!' she exclaimed in delight. 'When did you get back? I spoke to Beth on Saturday and she didn't say . . . '

'No, it was very late last night. I didn't bother her to pick us up. One of the other chaps gave us a lift from the airport.'

'Oh, I see. Well, Mum, how are you, and how was the tour?'

'Excellent—one of our best. Good audiences, and we were well received. Budapest was really fascinating.' Helen went into a glowing account of the places they had visited and people they had met.

Getting round to family matters at last, they spoke of Beth's surprise wedding plans and Joanna's father's latest marriage, and of Shaun's reappearance on her own scene.

'You're not going back with him, are you?' her mother said, unbelieving.

'No, but we're still friends. I see him from time to time. He does a Casualty day at the hospital. A number of the local GPs take their turn. And what's this I hear about you moving house?' Joanna went on.

'We-ell,' Helen paused, 'the fact is, love, Malcolm and I are getting a divorce.'

For a moment Joanna was dumbstruck. That was the last thing she had expected to hear. 'Oh, Mum!' she wailed. 'but I thought you and Malcolm were so happy?'

'So we were, at one time. But he's gone off the rails once too often, and enough is enough. We had a flaming bust-up just before Rachel's wedding actually, but we didn't want to spoil things for her, which is why we kept it quiet until now. Beth guessed, but I wanted to tell you myself.'

Joanna sighed. 'Oh dear! I *am* sorry. Are you very unhappy, Mum?'

'I was at first, naturally. But I'm getting over it now. He's leaving the Orpheus so we shan't be working together after this, which will help. When the house is sold I'm going to buy a flat in Hampstead—I've got my eye on one. You'll be able to come and stay whenever you like, and I shan't be lonely,' she went on brightly. 'I've got plenty of good friends.'

All the while her mother babbled on Joanna was still trying to come to grips with this latest turn in events. There was no doubt about her mother and father! Change was the name of the game, she thought despondently.

Presently she was obliged to call a halt to the

conversation and get ready for work. 'I'll have to go now, Mum, but I'll come down to see you on my next days off,' she promised. 'Give me another ring whenever you feel like a chat.'

Driving herself to the hospital, her spirits hit an all-time low. She had thought this third marriage of her mother's was for keeps. It had lasted longer than the others, and Joanna had always liked Malcolm. Why couldn't he have been faithful? Were men ever? Or was her mother just unlucky in her choice of partners?

Deep in thought she parked the car and entered the hospital through the Casualty entrance, where she came face-to-face with Giles as he emerged from the doctors' office. She didn't fancy talking to anyone at that moment, least of all him.

'Morning,' she said with a faint smile and would have walked on by.

He put out a hand to detain her, mild curiosity in his grey-green eyes. 'How are you, Joanna?'

She switched on what she hoped was a more convincing smile. 'I'm fine, thanks.'

'Judging by your sober face just now I was afraid your stars had bad news for you this morning,' he joked.

'I haven't seen a paper today, so I wouldn't know,' she returned in the same flippant fashion.

'Oh! I wondered if you were worried about our friend Lloyd?' He was more serious now. 'You've no need to be. He's under control, and most contrite in fact.'

She managed a light laugh. 'No, I'm not at all worried. Must go, or I'll be late. 'Bye,' and she hurried on before he asked more questions, knowing that her show of indifference hadn't really fooled him. Well, if he liked to imagine that Mr Lloyd was her problem, it was at least a feasible explanation.

Up on the ward Sister Judd confirmed what Giles had said about Mr Lloyd. 'If you'd rather avoid the man, I'll understand, but he's under control now. Do you know what his wife was bringing him in? Pure vodka . . . in a lemonade bottle! Luckily when we told her what had happened and asked about his drinking habits, she said she knew he was missing his booze and was it all right for him to have it?' The Sister shook her head in despair. 'Mr Beltane put her straight in no uncertain terms.'

Even so, later that afternoon Joanna started nervously when Mr Lloyd, making his unsteady way from the bathroom, confronted her. He was a large, heavy man and had he been fit would have been a formidable figure for anyone to tackle, let alone a slight girl.

'Oh! I didn't mean to make you jump, Nurse,' he said as she stepped back with a guarded look in her blue eyes. 'They tell me it was you I went for the other day when I flipped my lid . . . '

'Yes, it was,' she said.

'Duckie . . . I'm sorry about that,' he went on sheepishly. 'I wouldn't hurt any of you good girls for the world. I hope you're all right?'

'Yes, I'm okay, although you scared the living daylights out of me. Did you know you had a drink problem?'

'We-ell, I didn't realise that being without it would make me go round the bend. I'm going to try to ease up when I get out of here.'

'Best to get off it altogether, if you can. Talk to your own doctor . . . or try the AA.' With a smile of goodwill, Joanna went on her way to tea.

News of her experience had got around and in the staff canteen there were a number of enquiries as to her welfare, Steve amongst them.

One of the nurses from A & E said, 'We get our fair share of violence in Casualty, but we usually have a beefy porter around, or a security man.'

Steve puffed out his chest. 'She had GB and his merry men to come to the rescue, didn't she?'

'Thank heavens!' Joanna said with feeling.

That afternoon Sister Judd was on an early shift with her days off to follow.

'Mr Beltane has done his round,' she told Joanna, handing over the keys when she returned from tea. 'He's reduced Mr Lloyd's Heminevrin to two capsules six-hourly, and you're to call him immediately if there's any problem, but I don't think there should be. Oh! And a Dr Cassidy from A & E was asking for you. He didn't say why, only that he'd ring back later.'

The Sister looked curious, so Joanna felt obliged to explain. 'He's someone I used to know at my training hospital. He's fairly new to this district, and it's nice to meet a familiar face, isn't it?'

'Yes, I suppose so. One can't have too many friends,' Sister Judd returned.

During the visiting hour that evening Joanna,

glancing around the ward, saw that Mr Lloyd's wife was with him. She made a mental note to check later that no alcohol had been brought in, and then retired to the office to update her records. When the bell was rung at eight o'clock, however, Mrs Lloyd herself stopped by the office and put a box of chocolates on the desk.

'Tom asked me to give you these, Nurse,' she said. 'We're really terribly sorry for what happened the other day.'

'Oh, thanks!' Joanna smiled. 'Fortunately there was no real harm done.' She paused. 'You won't bring him in any alcohol, will you? Only he is on a drug to counteract his withdrawal symptoms.'

'Of course not, dear. I wouldn't dream of it now I've been told. Gosh! When I think about what he might've done, it gives me nightmares. You wouldn't think that going *without* it would drive a man crazy, would you?'

'Alcohol is a very addictive drug,' Joanna pointed out. 'Dependency can lead to the same problems as with all drugs.'

The woman nodded and sighed. 'I suppose you're right. It hasn't affected his operation, has it?'

'It won't have helped, although he seems to be making normal progress now. He's to have a special X-ray tomorrow to confirm that his bile duct is working properly. A cholangiogram we call it.'

'Yes, he was saying. What awful names you have for these things. You—er—won't hold this business against him, will you, Nurse?' Mrs Lloyd ventured, looking anxious. 'Only, I mean, it wasn't like Tom . . . '

'No, of course not,' Joanna reassured her. 'All we want is for him to get better.'

The woman sighed with relief. 'That's very sweet of you, thanks,' and she went on her way obviously glad to have cleared the air.

'Ooh! Goodies?' said Eunice, looking in on her way from the kitchen with the late-night drinks trolley. 'Well, that's better than a wreath!'

Joanna chuckled and stripped the wrapping off the box. 'I'll leave them here,' she said, 'tell everyone to help themselves.' Then she concentrated on writing her handover report.

At eight-thirty Shaun arrived in person and parked himself on the other chair in the office. 'Hallo,' he said perkily. 'What's this I hear about you being in the wars?'

'Was that why you rang—to enquire after my health?' Joanna asked sweetly.

'One of the reasons.'

'I'm touched by your concern!' she mocked. 'What was the other?'

'Seriously,' he leaned forward, took her hand and fondled it, 'are you okay?'

'Fine. You know me—I'm tough.'

His dark eyes twinkled. 'And as stubborn as they come! Now, my sweetheart, I want you to put yourself on an early on Thursday. You've got a dinner date with me.'

'Oh no, I haven't!'

'Jo!' he sighed, 'don't be difficult.'

'It's no good you badgering me, Shaun. I'll

never agree to marry you, or anyone else for that matter.'

'Well, all right, skip that for the moment. About Thursday, our senior partner is having a dinner party. All the other partners will have their wives there, and there'll be a couple of consultants with their better-halves I expect. I'll be like the spare one at the wedding. Help me out, please?'

She laughed. 'Oh, I see! Shaun at a loose end for a change. Okay, just for old times' sake. But don't read anything else into it.'

He ran his fingers through his dark curls and beamed triumphantly. 'I knew you wouldn't let me down.' His gaze turned to the doorway where Delphine, with a student nurse, had arrived to take over for the night. Letting his eyes wander over Delphine's trim figure and piquant features, he murmured, 'And who have we here?'

'This is Delphine,' Joanna said, 'France's contribution to the Common Market. Delphine, Dr Shaun Cassidy.'

' 'Allo!' Delphine said in her alluring sultry accent. ' 'Ow are you?'

'Enchanté, mam'selle!' Shaun replied, rising and bowing gallantly.

Joanna grinned. 'Well, would you like to practise your French somewhere else while we get on with the work?'

'I'll just sit here and be quiet until you've finished, then we'll go and have a quick one in the mess and make our arrangements, shall we?' he suggested.

'Please yourself.' She carried on and gave her report.

'Goodnight, Delphine,' Shaun smiled, when Joanna was at last ready to leave. 'I hope we shall meet again.'

She flashed her dark eyes at him and said: 'Do you work 'ere?'

'Oh, just on a part-time basis in A & E, but I'm in general practice locally. 'Bye for now.'

Joanna collected her bag and they walked over to the mess. 'She's a bit of all right, isn't she?' he said.

'The same old Shaun! I don't think there's any danger of *you* dying of a broken heart.'

After being served with their drinks, they found themselves a comfortable seat in an out-of-the-way corner. 'I'm not staying long,' she warned him. 'I've further to go now we live out at Pangbourne.'

'Oh, you've moved, have you? Well, that makes it more convenient for me to pick you up on Thursday . . . ' He stretched and sighed and gently massaged his midriff.

'What's the matter . . . indigestion?' Joanna asked.

'No, just a bit of gut rot. It'll go . . . I've taken something.' He went on to tell her a little about his colleagues and the practice set-up. 'They really are quite a decent bunch. Well married, of course, with families growing up or on the way. You'd fit in well.'

'What do you mean?' she laughed. 'I haven't got a family—or one on the way!'

'That could be arranged.'

She curbed a grin. 'You're hopeless.'

'No, just hopeful,' he bantered.

They exchanged addresses and telephone numbers and were on the point of leaving when Giles came in with another colleague. The doctors greeted each other.

'I hear you've been invited to my senior partner's "At Home" on Thursday,' Shaun said. He put his arm around Joanna's waist and gave her a squeeze. 'She's coming with me. We'll look forward to seeing you there.'

Giles gave her a brief, equivocal glance, eyebrows lifting slightly, and she thought his smile rather less than enthusiastic. 'Yes, it should be a good evening,' he murmured.

On the way home, Joanna felt even more depressed than she had that morning, what with her mother's talk of another marriage failure, and now Shaun landing her in a situation she would rather have avoided. He seemed to have a knack of doing that, although he wasn't to know how she felt about Giles. It was one thing to control her feelings at work, but socializing with the man was another matter.

On the other hand, it might not be a bad thing if Giles concluded there was still something between Shaun and herself. It might make him keep his distance, which would make life a great deal easier. She fell to wondering who he would be taking to the party . . . and worked up a most unreasonable dislike for whoever it might be.

On arriving back at the house she walked into the kitchen to find Gail on her knees, moist-eyed, sweeping up the pathetic remains of a blackbird which the cat had caught and brought in. 'Would you look at this?' she despaired. 'That little wretch!'

Joanna sighed and shuddered. 'Oh, what a shame. No wonder she doesn't eat her Pussykins.'

Gail popped out to the garden, tipped the remains of the songbird into the dustbin and came back and blew her nose. 'Well, we were warned, but it's one thing to hear about it and another to find the corpse in the kitchen.'

'The end of a perfect day!' Joanna mourned.

'Yes, I had a lousy session at the dentist's this morning. Cost me a bomb. And Tamsin's had the dismals all day because she's got to get out of her flat in a month,' Gail continued. 'Why, what went wrong for you?'

'Just about everything! My mother's back, she rang me after you left . . . and she's leaving Malcolm. I give up on my family.' Joanna spread her hands despairingly.

They made hot chocolate, cut into a fruit cake and gave vent to their respective moans.

'I've just let Shaun talk me into going to his senior partner's dinner party on Thursday. Wish I hadn't . . . I'll probably be bored to death.' She paused and made a face as a thought struck her. 'Hope he doesn't imagine he's taking me along to be vetted. You know he asked me to marry him . . . but I'm not falling for that!'

'Well, a dinner date won't commit you. Go and enjoy yourself, it might be a hoot.' Gail went on: 'About Tamsin . . . would you mind if I told her she could share my room? Not permanently, just until she can find something else.'

'No, of course not,' Joanna said. 'I like Tamsin, and there's plenty of room here, isn't there?'

'Okay. I'll tell her. That should improve the atmosphere in theatre tomorrow,' Gail said.

They went up to bed, where Joanna lay awake for ages, her brain over-active with the events of the day.

The human world, she brooded, was no kinder than the animal kingdom. People tore each other apart emotionally if not physically. As for Giles, the more she saw of him the more she hungered for him. After being nearly throttled by Mr Lloyd she had made all those noble resolutions about not hiding her true feelings and so on. But you couldn't go laying your heart at the feet of someone who didn't want it. A girl was entitled to her pride.

Destiny capriciously decided that Shaun would be taking no one to a dinner party in the near future. The following afternoon Joanna was asked to prepare a side ward for an emergency appendicectomy.

'It's one of our weekly clinicians,' said Charge Nurse John Masters, ringing her from A & E. 'Shaun Cassidy. Nice guy . . . do you know him?'

'Indeed I do. I was with him last night. He did mention he had a bit of an upset stomach,' Joanna remembered.

'Yes, I know he was feeling queasy yesterday, dosing himself with Mag. Trisil. Well, it looks like a full-blown abscess now. He's on his way to theatre. Giles thought it unwise to hang about.'

'Okay, John. We'll have the room ready.' Joanna put down the receiver and went to set wheels in motion. Poor Shaun, she thought. At the same time she experienced a sense of relief that the dinner date would now be off, and then was immediately guilt-stricken for being glad.

She was due off herself at four-thirty that day, which would leave Madge in charge. Madge was a married staff nurse who had recently returned to work after her youngest had started school.

'I've done all the paperwork,' Joanna told her as they folded the bedclothes into a theatre pack, put a transfusion stand in readiness and the post-anaesthetic equipment on the bedside cabinet.

'Crumbs!' Madge groaned, her kindly round face apprehensive, 'I hate looking after doctors. I always feel my performance is being assessed with a critical eye. And I'm a bit out of practice, let's face it.'

Joanna smiled. 'What a load of rubbish! You're doing fine. Anyway, lots of men prefer a mature nurse. And Shaun won't be difficult . . . he's a laidback sort of character—you'll like him.' She looked at her watch and handed over the ward keys. 'He should be up fairly soon. Think I'll hang on for a bit, I'd like to know how he is. I'll go down for him if you like?'

'All right, thanks, Jo. That would help.'

'Okay, I'll be in the staff room. Give me a call when he's ready.'

It was six o'clock when Madge looked in to say that the patient was ready for collection. Joanna replaced her cap which she had taken off while relaxing, and made her way down to theatre.

In the recovery room she found Dorian monitoring Shaun's safe return to consciousness. 'Hallo, there!' he said, blandly. 'Dr Cassidy's a friend of yours, that right?'

'Yes . . . how was it?' Joanna's brow furrowed as she looked down at the limp, inert figure of her erstwhile lover on the trolley.

'A bit messy, but Giles does a good job. He's had plenty of antibiotic cover, and he's boarded for Pethidine. Should be perking up in a couple of days.'

A febrile flush suffused Shaun's normally sallow cheeks. There was a nasogastric tube in one nostril and an intravenous infusion splinted to his forearm. 'Poor Shaun, he's going to know what it's like to be on the receiving end for a while,' she murmured sympathetically.

'Yes, a sobering experience,' Dorian agreed in his dry manner. 'Well, it's all up to you now. Take him away.'

She held the dextrose/saline drip aloft while the porters wheeled him to the lift and thence to the ward. Madge came to help settle him into his bed, and placing him on his side, they spread out the folded bedclothes and tucked him in.

'Hallo, Shaun!' Joanna spoke in a soothing voice, bending over him. 'It's all over. You're up on the ward now.'

His eyelids fluttered open, he muttered something she couldn't quite catch, and then closed them again. She smoothed the tousled dark hair back from his forehead, then checked his pulse. 'Ninety,' she said to Madge, and wrote it on the chart. 'They said it was rather messy . . . I expect the surgeons will be up to see him shortly. Well, I'll push off now. You'll be okay, will you?'

'Yes, fine. I'll get Beryl to look after him. Thanks for staying.'

Joanna collected her belongings from the staff room and made for the lift. As ever, her stomach flipped at the sight of Giles who came striding along the corridor, immaculate in a crisp white shirt and grey suit, dark hair neatly brushed.

'Hallo, what's this? Devotion beyond the call of duty?' he quipped, dark brows rising.

'Well, I wouldn't be much of a friend if I weren't concerned about him, would I?' she returned. 'Will he be all right?'

'Should be.' He stroked his chin thoughtfully. 'Where's that bright face you usually show the world? You're like a damp squib.'

She smiled wryly. 'One can't go around scintillating all the time. You should know that.'

He eyed her keenly. 'I must admit, life has been a bit fraught for you lately. How about if I appoint myself chief cheerer-upper?'

She looked into his intelligent and captivating face, and wondered if he knew that he was one of her problems. 'Oh, don't worry about me, I'm a survivor,' she said cheerfully, and she stepped into the lift which had arrived, and was borne away.

That man! He could pick up her moods like a finely-tuned radio. She'd like to bet he did know the effect he had upon her, much as she tried to hide it. Attractive men were not usually unaware of their charisma. Take his secretary, Tracy Kirk, for example, she gazed at him like an adoring spaniel, and he gave her the occasional pat on the head for her pains.

Joanna sighed and put him from her thoughts. Concentrate on your career, my girl! Work was the best way to forgetfulness.

Back at the house Gail was packing things into her car preparing to go home to Canterbury for her days off and her mother's birthday. 'See you Friday,' she said as Joanna waved her off. 'Don't forget to feed the carnivore!'

Left to her own devices Joanna relieved her pent-up feelings by Hoovering the living-room and tidying the kitchen and piling stuff into the washing machine, which was still a novelty.

Afterwards she cooked herself a meal of egg and tinned spaghetti, finished up with a chocolate bar and be blowed to the calories. Then she indulged in some lengthy phone calls with some of her old London workmates, and finally went to bed with the latest novel by her favourite thriller writer, Dick Francis.

Tonight, however, he failed to hold her attention and she fell asleep still hating the girl that Giles would be taking to the dinner party on Thursday.

CHAPTER ELEVEN

SHAUN made a remarkably good recovery from his perforated appendix. The day following his operation his infusion was able to be discontinued, his temperature fell to a less alarming level and some of his natural ebullience returned. Even though he complained in somewhat colourful language when the six-hourly antibiotics were jabbed into his buttocks, he rapidly won the hearts of the nursing staff on Paget Ward.

That afternoon, using the required aseptic technique, Joanna re-dressed his wound, shortening the drain as instructed.

'How's it looking . . . much exudate?' He raised his curly dark head, placing a hand on his abdomen, the better to see.

'Shaun! Take your hand away, for goodness' sake!' she scolded him. 'Do you want to get a Staph infection?'

He made a comic face at her. 'Okay, okay. Don't bully me. Carry on, my pet, you're doing a great job.'

She finished the dressing without further interference, tidied up and rearranged his pillows comfortably. 'Come on now, sit up a bit more, or you'll be getting a bad chest as well.'

As she leaned across to straighten the

bedclothes he planted a kiss on her cheek. 'You've the touch of an angel, my sweetheart. Sorry about our date tomorrow night. I'll make it up to you when I'm on my feet again.'

'Oh, forget it,' she smiled. 'I only agreed to go to oblige you.'

'Yes, I know.' A hint of the old roguish gleam crept into his dark eyes. 'Will Delphine be on tonight?'

'Why? Is she your number one target now?'

Shaun grinned. 'Well, I'm not making much headway with you, am I?'

Joanna ruffled his hair. 'You're incorrigible. You won't find Delphine the push-over I was, but the best of luck.' Pulling back the screening curtains, she poured him a drink, placed his locker within easy reach and left him to rest.

While she had been seeing to Shaun the doctors had arrived on the ward and were conferring with Sister Judd in the office before starting their round. Giles glanced in Joanna's direction as she wheeled her used trolley towards the clinical room. For a brief moment his magnetic eyes held hers and, predictably, rocked her composure. Feeling her colour rise, she gave him a brief smile of recognition and carried on her way.

With the first-shift staff nurse also on duty there was no call for Joanna to stop what she was doing and join the round, for which she was heartily glad. In time no doubt she would get over these tumultuous feelings he could stir in her, even with a glance; but for the moment her defences were fragile and she preferred to avoid him where possible.

Busying herself with routine tasks, she managed to stay out of contact until the doctors had departed. At four-thirty, taking over from Sister Judd for the rest of the day, she became totally absorbed with the needs of patients and getting everything shipshape for the night staff. And by the time she was ready to go off duty she was in a happier frame of mind.

There were no disturbing cases on the ward. About her mother's problem there was nothing she could do, except to listen if she wanted to talk, so there was no point in Joanna agonizing over that. In any case, as Giles had said, her parents were old enough to look after themselves. But she was not going to think about Giles, either, was she?

It was a beautiful summer's evening as she stepped out to the car-park en route for home. The sort that made one glad to be alive. She flung her cap in the back of the car, ran her fingers through her blonde hair and shook it free, feeling cheerful and optimistic.

Her whole life was before her, uncluttered, to do exactly as she pleased. Now that she hadn't got to go to that dinner party with Shaun tomorrow evening she would be able to go to the new aerobics class advertised on the staff notice board. There had also been talk amongst the A & E crowd of hiring a house-boat for their next disco get-together, which sounded great. Then, with Beth's wedding coming up quite soon, she would have to buy a new outfit for that. Who needed the hassle and complications of love when there was so much else to do?

Back at the house Joanna skipped up to her room and discarded her uniform for a pair of white cotton trousers and a loose, blue check shirt. It was nearly ten p.m., still not dark, and the setting sun was painting the sky in glorious shades of flame.

Downstairs she opened the french windows into the garden and wandered out, feeling at peace with the world. On the fence the pink roses were luminous and fragrant in the evening air. She was bending her head to smell them when the sound of someone at the side-gate caused her to look up, and her heart lurched to find Giles standing there.

'I did try the front doorbell,' he said, grinning at her surprise.

She swallowed, feeling breathless at the sight of him. Six feet of rugged masculinity, outrageously seductive and alarmingly lovable, sending ripples of desire racing through her body. 'H-hallo . . . what are you doing here?' she said.

'I'm looking for the survivor.'

Joanna smiled apprehensively. 'How did you know where to find me?'

'A few simple enquiries. May I come in?'

'Please do . . . I was just going to make coffee.' She led the way into the living-room and turned to face him. 'Is this just a social call . . . or what?'

'Yes, I suppose you could call it that,' he returned, scratching his cheek thoughtfully. 'The thing is, since your dinner date for tomorrow is confined to bed, I decided I should offer to take you myself.'

'Oh, that. It's all right, I'm glad not to be going. I mean, it's hardly the event of the year,' she laughed, 'the local GPs and their wives!'

She had to keep talking to quell her rising panic. He was too near, and looking at her in a way that set her senses haywire. 'Thanks all the same, but as a matter of fact, I'd already decided to go to aerobics instead . . . '

'*Aerobics!*' he cut in, in a comic voice. 'Come on, you can't pass up an evening of my company for a session of physical jerks.'

'Why can't I?' Joanna said indignantly. 'Anyway, who were you supposed to be taking until now? Have you been let down?'

'No, I haven't been let down. I was on the point of asking *you* earlier, but your talkative friend got there ahead of me.'

Joanna's blue eyes widened. 'Oh! Really?'

'Yes. I could have garrotted that goddam Irishman,' Giles said forcefully.

She giggled. 'A good thing he didn't know, or he wouldn't have felt too happy to have you put the knife in.'

'I should have liked to do much, much more than remove his appendix!' he growled. 'Look, can I take it that there is nothing special between you two?'

'I told you so ages ago.'

'Then you and I have some talking to do.' He reached for her hands and pulled her to him. For a long moment their eyes held, and it was as though they were poised on the brink of some predestined happening. Neither of them spoke, but there was no need. She knew what was coming before his arms closed about her, and when his seeking mouth claimed hers, she had no will or wish to resist. She melted against him, all her fine resolutions forgotten as he kissed her with a deeply possessive passion, releasing all the pent-up desire that had been building in her for so long.

This was how she had dreamed it would be with Giles—breathtaking and magical, blotting out everything else but the glorious now. And if it were to be only a transient affair she didn't even care any more. She'd got over Shaun, hadn't she? She'd proved that infatuation passes. The trouble was, she had never felt quite this way about Shaun . . .

Presently Giles held her away, cupped her chin in his hands and studied her upturned face earnestly. 'Now, are you well and truly kissed into submission?'

'No,' she said with a tremulous laugh, 'and that's not what I call talking.'

'*That* was to put you in the right frame of mind for what I have to say,' he countered, a smile lurking at the corners of his mouth.

'Oh dear, this all sounds very serious. Sh-shall we sit down . . . ' The way her own limbs were feeling, it was a case of having to.

They sat together on the sofa, their bodies brushing, the atmosphere between them supercharged. Joanna's heart was pounding, her tension almost unbearable in the silence which followed.

'Well?' she said, feeling her cheeks flame, knowing he must be aware of how she felt about him, and not knowing exactly what was in his mind.

'Joanna . . . ' He lifted one of her hands and kissed it, 'when my wife died I decided to close the book on love. I could do without that kind of trauma again. And I was doing fine until a certain blue-eyed blonde came along and upset the apple-cart.' He paused and gave a self-mocking smile.

'Giles Beltane—the man who needed no one! Yet whenever I saw you with Cassidy I felt furious. It could only be jealousy, much as I hated to admit it. Then that lunatic on the ward tried to strangle you, and . . . well . . . I couldn't bear the thought of life without you.'

He put his hands on her shoulders, his eyes searching hers. 'I love you, Joanna. I need you. I want you. Will you marry me?'

She caught her breath, not far from tears as both happiness and heartache overwhelmed her. 'Oh, Giles,' she murmured, 'I love you too. But . . . aren't I a terrible marriage risk? Look at my parents—six marriages between them.' Her lips trembled. 'And there's m-my mother about to get another divorce. Th-there seems to be a jinx on long-term relationships in our family.'

'So that's what's been on your mind lately.' He stroked back her hair and kissed her brow. 'You're an amazing girl, you know. You *are* a survivor. You battle on despite the knocks, still loving people, getting on with what has to be done . . . '

She gave a watery smile and shook her head. 'The private me is just as mixed up as the rest of the family. Must be something in my genes.'

'Don't talk rubbish. You said yourself that you're the odd one out.' He caught her to him, saying vehemently, 'To hell with other people—we can make a go of it, I know we can.'

It was an earth-moving experience to relax in his arms, to be caressed and kissed with a forcefulness that lifted her to heights of ecstasy. 'I love you . . . love you . . . love you,' he murmured huskily.

The moment was interrupted by a metallic click, and a pale bundle of fur streaked across the room and ran up the curtains.

Giles glanced up. 'What on earth was that?'

The cat peered down at them with winking blue eyes. 'That's Willow,' Joanna told him. 'She's naughty. She catches birds.'

'Oh!' He turned his attention back to her, his eyes twinkling. 'Have I caught mine?'

She laughed softly. 'I was caught long before you asked me. But you knew that, didn't you?'

'Did I?' He pressed a finger on her nose. 'I can be very discreet.'

She nestled against his broad chest and sighed dreamily. 'I can't believe this is all for real. Is it? You did ask me to marry you?'

'I did indeed. Still need convincing, do you?' He set about doing so in a manner which left her in no doubt at all, and it was utter bliss to be crushed to his powerful body while he kissed her as though he could never love her enough.

'Satisfied now?' Giles murmured tenderly, his lips still teasing hers.

Her eyes were starry. 'Mmmm . . . but it still seems like a fairy-tale.'

'All fairy-tales end . . . *and they lived happily ever after,* so what more can you want?'

And it was true. She could wish for nothing more than the precious gift of his love and the exquisite pleasure of sharing her life with his for ever.

'Now, I don't believe in long engagements, my darling, so we had better start making plans,' he went on.

'Yes, darling,' she agreed submissively, wreathing her arms around his neck and kissing him again. Which of course delayed the plan-making for some considerable time.

A marriage for romance or revenge?

Twenty-one years ago Mario di Medici was murdered at sea. Many suspected it was James Tarleton's hand that had pushed him over the rail.

When his daughter, Chris Tarleton, came to Venice, the riddle of the past returned with her.

Before she knew how, she found herself married to Marcus di Medici, the dead man's son.

Was his marriage proposal intended to protect her from the shadowy figure that followed her every move?

Or was his motive revenge?

W**()**RLDWIDE

Another title from the Worldwide range.